LIKE A RIVER

LIKE A RIVER

A Civil War Novel

Kathy Cannon Wiechman

CALKINS CREEK
AN IMPRINT OF HIGHLIGHTS
Honesdale, Pennsylvania

Text copyright © 2015 by Kathy Cannon Wiechman
Jacket illustration copyright © 2015 by Christopher Silas Neal

All rights reserved
For information about permission to reproduce selections from this book,
contact permissions@highlights.com.

Although this work centers on historical events, this is a work of fiction.
Some of the characters are based on real individuals, but most names,
characters, and incidents are products of the author's imagination and are
used fictitiously. Any resemblance to actual incidents or persons, living or
dead, is entirely coincidental.

Calkins Creek
An Imprint of Highlights
815 Church Street
Honesdale, Pennsylvania 18431

Printed in the United States of America
ISBN: 978-1-62979-209-5
Library of Congress Control Number: 2014945289

First edition
The text of this book is set in Weiss.
Design by Barbara Grzeslo
Production by Margaret Mosomillo
10 9 8 7 6 5 4 3 2 1

*Dedicated to the memory of my mother, Thea B. Cannon
and in tribute to prisoners of war*

PART ONE

LEANDER

1
RIVER OF WORDS

"WHAT DID YOU SAY?" PA'S VOICE BOOMED.

Fifteen-year-old Leander watched his older brother fidget the way he always did when Pa's voice got loud and his eyes seemed louder. He saw Nate's gaze drop to the untouched chicken on his plate. Leander winced as Nate winced, knowing how it felt to be the object of Pa's scrutinizing look.

Pa coughed and cleared his throat, his eyes never leaving Nate's face. *Go ahead, Nate,* Leander thought. He needed to hear the words again, too. Words impossible to believe from just one telling.

Nate looked up slowly. He tugged at his collar the way Leander had often seen him do at school when Miss Dobbs called on him to recite or solve a problem in long division.

"I said me and Given are going to join the army." Nate's shaky voice got a tad more firm by the last word.

"The army?" Pa questioned.

"Yes, sir," Nate said, his voice gathering its firmness and making the words strong. "President Lincoln needs men to replace what was lost at Gettysburg last month. I'm eighteen now, and it's what I want . . . what I need to do."

Leander couldn't believe it. Nate had never mentioned the army before, at least not in front of *him*. When had he and Given planned this? Why hadn't Nate told him? Had Given told *his* family yet? Did Lila know?

A bite of biscuit remained in Leander's mouth. He had forgotten to chew or swallow, as he waited for Pa's next words, but the words that filled the air were Ma's.

"Do you know how many soldiers have died already? Thousands at Gettysburg."

Pa cleared his throat again. "The Rebs are on the run since Lee's retreat at Gettysburg. Could be a Union victory is close, but they'll need good soldiers." He threw back his shoulders and said, "I'll be proud to have you in the great forces from Ohio."

A smile spread across Nate's face, but Ma stood up and cleared the supper dishes.

"Ma!" Leander cried, as his plate was snatched from in front of him. "I wasn't finished."

But Ma didn't say a word. Not one word.

Pa and Nate moved to the porch, and Leander followed.

"We reckoned we'd sign up next week," Nate said.

"Next week!" Leander said. "You're going next week?"

Pa said, "Your chores finished, Leander? Birdie can't milk herself."

"But—"

Pa's eyebrows arched and his eyes said *No buts*, even though his mouth said nothing.

Leander hurried to the small grazing pasture, where the red-brown cow was tied to her picket pin. The smell of a fresh cow pie warned him to watch his step. Flies buzzed around the manure, and when a few of them rose to Birdie's tail, she swished it twice, and they went back to the cow pie.

Birdie turned her head to glance at Leander for one blink before she went back to chewing. Leander felt of no more consequence than the flies, dismissed with a swish— barely a rung above the manure itself. Akin to the way Pa and Nate made him feel.

He tugged Birdie's pin from the ground and led her to the barn, where dusty hay and smelly manure created a scent Leander had come to like. He lifted the tin pail from its hook inside the barn door, filled Birdie's feedbox with three scoops from the oat bin, and plunked himself on the milking stool.

Between squirts of milk zinging into the pail, quiet murmurs reached Leander's ears. Pa's and Nate's voices, voices that made Leander feel younger than the three-year difference between him and Nate. He wanted to be part of that conversation with Pa and Nate, wanted Pa to treat *him* like a man, too.

"Nate and Giv are going to be soldiers in the army," he complained to Birdie. "They'll go clean down South to fight Rebels. But I got to stay here like a young'un. Only time Pa pays *me* any mind is when he wants me to work harder."

He lugged the full pail to the cool cellar and covered it with a cloth to keep out flies. He slipped through the kitchen, heading for the porch, but Ma stopped him, told him to wash up and get ready for bed.

"It ain't even dark yet."

"Now." Ma was usually lenient about summer bedtime when the daylight hung on longer, but her disposition had been soured by Nate's words at supper.

Leander washed all the way to the backs of his ears and headed toward the loft ladder. Ma was at the table, her head in her hands, her shoulders quivering.

Leander reached his arms around her in a hug. "Don't worry, Ma," he said. "He'll come back."

She patted his arm and looked up at him with wet eyes.

He smiled. "And you still got me."

He climbed the ladder to the loft room he shared with Nate, but he didn't put on his nightshirt. He sat on the edge of the narrow windowsill and tried to hear Pa and Nate.

From the window, he saw the same gentle hills as every day. Even in the waning sunlight, his eyes sorted out summer's greens and yellows, knowing the cornfields from the oats. He knew which greens were beeches and hickories, and where the tallest oak stood. And far in the distance, where a hint of fog tinged the greens, was the river, the mighty Ohio. He couldn't see the water from here, but he knew exactly where it was. He often stood on the riverbank, gazing across to where Kentucky was close enough to be houses and chimney smoke.

Some folks at church had kin in Kentucky, but others thought Kentuckians were near as bad as Rebel

Confederates because they held with keeping slavery legal. Now Nate was going to join the Union Army and fight against those Rebels.

But from this window, everything looked the same. For some reason, Leander had expected something different—different like Nate and Pa. And Ma, too.

He had always liked listening to Ma and Pa's conversations, which flowed like a river. Their words, like streams and rain and runoff, added to the conversation and carried it far from where it began. Sometimes their words meandered slowly, sometimes built to a torrent, but they always traveled together—until Nate's announcement dropped into their river of words like a huge tree, its trunk and branches refusing to let the flow continue. Now it had dried up completely.

Now Pa's words were with Nate, leaving Leander aside like a child with his ear pressed against the windowpane.

2

THE POND

LEANDER DIPPED HIS FISHHOOK IN AND OUT OF the water, impatience lapping at his innards. He was tired of waiting for Nate to bring up the army.

Why was it so hard to talk to this new grown-up Nate who had changed everything? *Why do you want to leave?* was what Leander wanted to ask, but what he said was, "They sure ain't biting today, are they?"

"You trying to catch a fish or drown that earthworm?" Nate said, sounding like his same-old big-brother self.

"Giv's not fishing today?" Leander asked, determined to wade into talk about last night.

"He and his pa are patching their barn roof, getting the place ready for when he ain't here."

"Are his folks takin' on as bad as Ma is? About you two joining up?"

"Ma'll see things Pa's way sooner or later," Nate said. "You know how they are."

Leander had thought he knew, but this morning Ma had set Pa's breakfast plate on the table with a clunk—and that plate said more than she did. Pa barely seemed to notice, and Ma rattled pans and clinked dishes all through breakfast.

Now Leander perched with Nate on the bank of their pond, his hook in the water, but his mind feeling *under*water. His thoughts swam back and forth between Nate's leaving and Ma and Pa's being near as split as the Union and the Rebs. Surely they would talk again soon. They had the kind of marriage Leander always reckoned he and Lila would have one day. He had a whole heap to tell Lila next time he saw her.

But now Nate was the one he spoke to. "Home won't seem right without you."

Nate turned to give his brother a hard look. "I'll be gone before harvest, Lee. Pa's going to need you to do the work of a man."

Those weren't the words Leander wanted to hear. "I always do, Nate, but you and Pa seem blind to it."

Nate squeezed his eyes into a tight squint. "What you work hardest at is getting out of working hard."

"Ain't true," Leander defended. "I help Pa and do my own chores, too. I take care of the chickens and milk Birdie twice a day."

"Milking Birdie ain't hard. She *gives* her milk more than you have to *take* it."

"I help in the barn, too."

Being tall and long-armed like Pa, Nate never understood. Leander was small like Ma's kin. Nate didn't know how hard it was to shovel manure with a pitchfork whose handle stood taller than Leander. Why did Nate have to pick on him now? Now, when they only had a sliver of time left together?

He bit back his anger. "I try, Nate. I surely try."

Leander's eyes scanned the pond. He'd always thought the pond's shape resembled their old sow Hazel, named for the hazelnut-shaped mark just behind her neck. On a day when the water was still and the sun just right, he could see the rock shelf that looked like that mark, jutting out below the surface of the pond.

The best morning fishing was usually along the pig's belly, where the water ran deep. Closer to noontime, they might move to the pig's neck because fish liked to hide under the rock shelf. But today, fish weren't biting anywhere. The sun peeked over the treetops, and Leander's line seemed to end at the sunlit shimmer on the water.

Nate jerked in his line. "Dang critter wiggled hisself off the hook."

"The fish don't need our bait," Leander snapped, still feeling prickly over Nate's insult. "Too many pond skaters today." He watched the skinny brown bugs skim across the surface and tried to let his mind catch hold of yesterday and return life to what it had always been. But yesterday was even harder to catch than fish.

"Why you got to leave, Nate?" Leander's light punch to his brother's shoulder might have been a little harder than his usual teasing.

"Some things are worth fighting for." Nate had never been outspoken about the war, but now he talked like he was ready to pick up arms and fight. "It's what I got to do," Nate went on. "The Army's paying a signing bounty, and I'd earn fifteen dollars a month to boot."

"You doing this for money? Why you need all that money?"

"For my future, so's I can make real plans."

"You're tetched, Nate. You're gonna go and get shot at to make money?"

"Like I said, some things are worth fighting for."

August's heat was burning the morning into a steamy day, and Leander wiped his sweaty face on his sleeve.

Nate dropped his line on the bank. "It's too hot to fish," he said and slithered out of his clothes right down to his drawers. "Last one in eats Jeff Davis's eye pus," he called out and flung himself into the pond with a splash.

Leander joined him quick as one of those pond-skating bugs. Swimming had always come easy to Leander, and he caught up to Nate and gave him a playful shove.

They splashed each other, and Nate pulled Leander under the surface by the seat of his drawers. Leander returned with a push on Nate's head. They'd played in the pond this way since they were boys, and Leander had a deep catch in his chest knowing this might be the last time the two of them would play like children.

Panting hard, they lolled on their backs in the cool water. Leander closed his eyes against the bright sunlight and felt the water lapping against him. Splashing sounds around his ears eased him and tried to comfort the turmoil in his mind.

He thought ahead to the day Nate and Given would march off. Ma would be in tears and leaning on Pa—if they were speaking to one another. Surely, Ma and Pa would go back to the way things had always been between them. And with Nate away, maybe Pa would finally pay heed to his second son.

Giv's family would be there, of course, including his sister, Lila. She'd be heart-wrenched, and it would seem right for Leander to put his arm around her shoulders and pat her hand. Even though he and Lila had always been as close as two drops of dew on the same leaf, he never seemed to fire up the courage to touch her the way he did in his dreams, dreams where he even kissed her.

He hoped she knew that he planned to marry her one day. That plan had lived deep inside him since the day they'd gigged frogs on the bank of this very pond. Lila hadn't cringed or squealed the way most girls did when he pierced the frog's skin with the gigging stick. When she'd gigged her own frog and held it up for Leander's inspection, her buck-toothed grin stretching her lips wide, he had fallen headlong in love with her.

He loved her now more than ever, now that Lila had grown into the prettiest girl in Lawrence County, Ohio. They walked to school together every day, side by side, barely a breath of air between their shoulders. It didn't matter that her shoulder rode higher than his. She never made him feel small.

Something stirred in Leander when he thought of Lila, the smell of her, the laugh in her teasing blue eyes, the lips that revealed a woman's smile where the buck teeth had once been.

Being there to comfort Given's sister might finally give him the chance to show her how he felt, maybe even say the words he had kept tucked inside himself all these years. And she would say she felt the same way, wouldn't she?

3

LILA

W

"HAT YOU BOYS THINK YOU'RE DOING?"

Leander's eyes flew open when he heard Lila's voice. Startled, he planted his feet too quickly on the muddy bottom of the pond, and they slipped out from under him. He clutched at the surface, gasping for a breath that was more water than air. When he found his feet again and came up coughing and spitting water, Nate and Lila were laughing.

"You swimming or drowning?" Lila teased.

"I'd like to see you do better," Leander called to her, watching her stand on the bank with her hands on her hips.

Lila's hair, the color of autumn grasses, framed her face like sunshine. "Do better? Why, I could swim deeper than a catfish and faster than either one of you—if I had a mind to."

"Like to see you try," Nate dared her.

"You think I won't?"

"Just said I'd like to see you try."

"Maybe I will, but turn your heads first, both of you."

Leander turned his head, but the corner of his eye caught her movements as Lila undid the fastenings on her dress and peeled it off. She hung it over the low branch of a maple tree before she slipped off her petticoat, or whatever furbelows girls wore under their dresses. When he heard a splash, he turned to see her plowing through water up to her pinky-white shoulders, beautiful shoulders covered by a flimsy layer of feminine frill. Leander's eyes followed down the cleft in her neck to where the water lapped against her skin. He was glad most of him was underwater and that the water was cold.

Nate swam toward Lila, but she stood firm and gave him her you-don't-scare-me look. He edged past her and eased into the shallow water of the pig's back with a mischievous set to his chin. Lila pretended to cover her eyes, but made a show of leaving a gap between her fingers. She stared openly as Nate slogged up the muddy bank, his wet drawers dripping down his legs.

"Lila McGlade, have you no shame?" he called out, standing halfway up the slope with his drawers clinging to him like moss to a cluster of damp rocks.

Lila's face reddened and Nate grinned, staring at her hard until she looked away.

He got a running start down the slope, his unwavering gaze on Lila, and hurled himself into the air like buckshot from Pa's shotgun. He plunged feet-first into the pond somewhere near the pig's neck, and splashes rippled toward Lila and Leander like a taunt.

Leander waited for him to break the surface, but the wait grew long. He readied himself for a tug at his ankles, for Nate to pull him under, but there was no tug. He looked at the spot where his brother had gone in and wondered where he might have swum to. How long had Nate been underwater? It seemed like minutes—long, long minutes.

"Stop it, Nate!" he called out, but no laughing Nate came up for air. Leander's eyes followed the edge of the bank, looking for a place Nate might have climbed out to hide and scare them. He saw nothing.

"You're not funny, Nate," Lila said, a pout on her lips, but fear in her eyes.

How close to the rock shelf had Nate jumped? He'd been watching Lila instead of where he was going. Leander's skin went gooseflesh, and he stroked through the water toward the spot where Nate had gone in, sure that any second Nate would show himself and gloat over the scare he'd given them. But there was no sign of him. No sign until Leander bumped into the underwater rock shelf and a large *something* beneath its edge. Not a something! A someone! It was Nate. Leander grabbed Nate's hair and pulled him up. But the water tried to suck him back down.

"Nate!" he pleaded to the weight that pulled against the handful of hair, still hoping Nate would shake his head and laugh.

Lila's scream pierced the air as she thrashed toward them.

Leander grabbed Nate under his arms and pulled him from under the shelf and toward the bank. When he reached shallow water, Lila grabbed an arm and tugged along with him, her face frantic, her breath coming in gasps. Nate's body lay heavy in their grasp.

Don't be dead. Leander tried to will life back into Nate with his silent plea. *Don't be dead. Please don't be dead.*

4
LIVE, NATE, LIVE!

L EANDER LAID NATE FACEDOWN AND POUNDED on his back. He rolled him onto his side and pushed on his belly.

"Come on, Nate, breathe!" Tears and pond water ran down Leander's face as he pushed harder.

Finally Nate gurgled and coughed. And gasped. And breathed.

Leander breathed, too. He hadn't realized he'd been holding his breath until he let the air out again.

Nate's breathing was loud and labored, and Leander tried to help him to sit up, but Nate cried out in pain and his legs lay as limp as near-empty sacks of seed.

Leander jumped to his feet. "I'll fetch Pa. You stay with Nate," he told Lila, trying not to notice how her wet underthings clung to the feminine roundness of her body. "And put your clothes on," he called over his shoulder as he hurried up the slope.

Leander rushed past the vegetable patch, his eyes searching it for Pa. He called "Pa!" into the dim interior of the barn. Just as Pa stepped from between the tall stalks of the cornfield, Given McGlade ran around the corner of the house.

"I was up on the barn roof, saw you drag Nate outta the swimming hole," Given said, breathless. "Is he alive?"

Leander nodded. "Barely."

Pa gasped and hurried with Giv down the hill to the bank of the pond. Leander followed, his bare feet scarcely feeling the pebbles strewn along the slope.

Lila sat on the ground with Nate's head in her lap. Only half her buttons were buttoned and the wetness of her underthings bled through her dress.

Pa spoke to Nate in an even voice that didn't match the fearful look on his face. "Lie easy, son. Don't try to talk. You're going to be fine."

Pa stood back, and Given lifted Nate as easily as Leander could lift a pillow. But pillows never cried out the way Nate did. Nate's eyes rolled back and closed as Given laid him across his broad shoulder and carried him up the hill.

Lila followed close behind and pleaded with Nate not to die. Pa's tight face looked to Leander for answers, but Leander's mouth wouldn't form words.

Ma asked frantic questions as Given and Pa gently settled Nate in her and Pa's bed.

Leander tried to clear his head and drew in a mouthful of air. "He jumped in the pond on the run and never came up. Must've hit the rock shelf."

Pa blew out his breath.

"Leander got him breathing again," Lila added.

Pa patted Leander's shoulder, then gripped it tightly. Leander felt the shaking in his father's grasp.

Given left to fetch Doc Marting, and Ma took over. She ran a tied rag of herbs under Nate's nose until his eyelids fluttered and opened. While they waited for the sound of Doc's buggy, Nate drifted in and out of sleep. When awake, he screamed out in pain, screams that sent chills deep into Leander.

★ ★ ★

The doctor said Nate's leg bones had been shattered when he struck the rock shelf. He said they must take great care to keep infection from setting in. He handed Ma a tin of powder and instructed her how to mix it with water to ease Nate's pain.

Doc laid wooden splints against Nate's legs and wrapped them in heavy sacks to keep them from moving. Leander didn't see how Nate could move them anyway. They didn't look like real legs anymore; more like two huge pale worms with no bones inside.

When Pa raised Nate's head for Ma to give him his medicine, Nate's face scrunched from pain and a sharp whimper escaped his lips. After Ma dribbled some of the powder-and-water mixture into his mouth, putting his head back on the pillow brought a wail. Leander wondered if Nate could survive this—and would he want to?

As Leander headed up the ladder to his loft room, he looked back and saw Ma leaning against Pa, Pa's arm circling her waist. Leander had thought he'd do anything to see them close again, but why, why did it have to be because of this?

5
NURSE LILA

MA TENDED NATE DAY AND NIGHT, AND most every day the doctor came to check on him, looking him over for signs of infection. Mrs. McGlade brought meals for them. "Easy enough to cook for two broods as it is for one," she said.

Ma looked heart-and-bone-tired, her face carved with worry lines. Leander fretted over both her and Nate. Even Lila tried to help, to give Ma a chance to rest. The morning after that terrible day, Leander found Lila asleep in the chair beside Nate's bed.

"Ain't you been home yet?"

She shook her head. "I stayed to help."

And she stayed. Hour after hour, bathing Nate's face with cloths, feeding him from a spoon, fetching and carrying like a servant, cooing like a mother dove.

Leander felt grateful for Lila's help—at first. But watching the way she fawned over Nate began to nip at him. When he tried to talk to her, she nudged him away or slushed him so Nate could sleep. Every bit of her sweetness was spent on Nate, and Leander felt like a neglected dog.

Nate rarely spoke except to ask for more medicine, a drink of water, a bite to eat. Ma or Lila hurried to fetch what he wanted.

A very small speck in the back of Leander's mind was *almost sorry* he'd pulled Nate out of the pond. But he never let that speck stay long. He wanted Nate well again as much as anyone.

★ ★ ★

After Nate had lain in bed for three weeks with no sign of infection, Doc Marting let up on his regular visits.

"I have other patients to tend to," he said. "It's a wonder, but the boy should live a long life."

"Thank God," Ma said, clasping her hands together.

When Ma walked the doctor to the door, he paused, adjusted his spectacles, and looked at her and Pa and Leander. "He's going to live," he repeated, "but he's never going to walk again."

31

6
CHANGES

LEANDER REMEMBERED HOW NATE'S ANNOUNCE-ment about the army had changed Ma and Pa. But Nate's accident changed everything. Even the air felt different, as though no one in the house breathed quite so easily anymore.

Ma had always had a soft spot for Leander, but now caring for Nate took a large bite from her time and patience. Leander had to do Nate's chores as well as his own, including pulling weeds from the vegetable patch, weeds with stubborn roots that refused to let go. He never seemed to work quickly or thoroughly enough to suit Ma.

Nearly two months passed before Pa lifted Nate from the bed for the first time. Pa settled him onto a chair by the window, so he could see out. Ma made up a bed for Nate in the kitchen, since he could no longer climb the loft ladder.

Sleeping alone in the loft, Leander didn't have the sound of Nate's stirrings in the morning to wake him. If Ma had to call him twice, she was bound to snap at him.

Without Nate to help with the harvest, Leander had to work harder than ever. Given often came to help. Mr. McGlade earned a good living as a cobbler, making shoes for half of Lawrence County, so the McGlades didn't plant as many fields as the Jordans did. They didn't have to depend on their small farm for each bite they put into their mouths.

Pa never let up on Leander while they worked. "You don't need to stop for water after each row, son. A man has to keep going." But Pa's long legs didn't have to work as hard as Leander's short ones. Trying to keep up made him thirsty, and taking time for a drink let him catch his breath.

One thing hadn't changed. No matter how long Leander kept going, how tired he got, how much his arms and legs ached, he never saw a look of pride on Pa's face like the one he'd had for Nate. Every evening, Leander came into the house with his face, hair, and clothes wet with the sweat of hard work.

"You ain't lettin' Pa and Giv do all the back-bustin', are you, Lee?" Nate called one day from his chair by the window.

"I didn't sit on my hindquarters the way someone did." Leander was sorry for the words the second he spoke them, even before Nate's face showed the sting of them. Leander knew how tough life had become for Nate. He watched every morning as Pa carried Nate from bed to chair. He witnessed the grimace that gripped Nate's face and heard the groans that escaped his lips.

He put his hand on Nate's shoulder. "I didn't mean it, Nate, I swear."

Nate reached up and laid his hand atop his brother's, letting his fingers do the forgiving. "Giv's leaving after harvest," Nate said. "Next spring, you won't have his help with the fieldwork."

"Giv's still joining up?"

"Of course. He stayed long enough for me to get through the worst, and by then he reckoned you and Pa needed him."

"So even Giv didn't think I was man enough to handle the work? Did you ask Lila for her thinking, too?"

"Lila knows you as well as the rest of us. You just got some growing up to do, little brother."

Leander peeled off his sweat-soaked shirt and flung it across the back of a chair. He'd toiled in the fields every day, worked harder than ever before. Pa hadn't noticed, and neither had Nate. He was fifteen years old—fifteen-and-a-half! How many years did it take to be treated like a man?

* ★ *

On the last day of harvest, when haystacks dotted the hayfield and the rest of the crops were stored in the barns and cribs and cellar, Given came to the house.

"I'm heading to Holderby's Landing in the morning," he said. "Since West Virginia became a state, Union recruiters are over there looking for new men."

"I know you planned to do this in August," Pa said, gripping Given's hand and giving it a manly shake. "We appreciate your staying to help us out."

"God keep you safe," Ma said, grasping him in a hug.

"I'll see you again before I leave for muster," Giv said.

Leander followed him to the door. "You going clean across the river to join?" The other side of the river had stared back at Leander all his life. Holderby's Landing was on the edge of West Virginia that leaned up against Kentucky. It seemed to call to him. "I've always wanted to cross the river, Giv. Can I go with you?"

Given looked at Ma for approval.

Ma nodded. "The harvest is in. A day off might be good for him—if you don't mind, Given?"

Leander smiled a thank-you to Ma, deep down clinging to an idea that was hatching in his brain. He'd show them who was a man. He'd show them all.

7

THE FERRY

L EANDER'S IDEA FESTERED IN HIS MIND ALL
night. One minute he feared he couldn't go through with
it; the next, he swore he had to. With everything in the
house changed, it was time to make his own change. It
would be hard on Ma and Pa for sure, but they had driven
him to it, hadn't they?

The next morning, Ma didn't have to call him even
once. He was dressed, had his chores finished, and was
ready for breakfast before the sun had cleared the horizon.

Leander reached the McGlade house as Given was
climbing up to sit beside his pa on the cobbler wagon seat.
The two broad-shouldered men filled the seat, so Leander
had to ride inside.

During the ride, he dodged the maple lasts that Mr.
McGlade used for making shoes. The misshapen, toeless,

wooden feet hung beside him and clattered against one another as the wagon bumped along the river road. Leander refused to let the sound distract his resolve. His decision was made.

When Mr. McGlade reined in his mare at the ferry landing, Leander unfolded his legs and climbed from the wagon. The Ohio rushed by as though it were being chased, and he took a deep breath of the wet river smell. Mr. McGlade promised to return by the time they got back and drove off to tend to his cobbler business.

The ferry was part-raft, part-steamboat, tethered to posts on the bank like a critter trying to break free. Leander and Given paid their fares and stepped aboard.

A man at the long tiller arm nodded to them, and Leander felt the river's strength beneath him. Could the man see the shivers that crept up Leander's legs? He had stood on the riverbank many times, waded into shallow water along its edge, but now he floated atop it like the steamboats and rafts he had watched so often.

The ferry slowly chugged from the Ohio shore and out into the river, rocking up and down with the water's movement. Leander knew the river's force could pull the ferry downriver or tumble them into its water. He gripped a rail to keep his balance.

Given's hands were in his pockets. He was taller than Pa, and folks had treated him like a man since he was ten years old. Leander remembered the way Pa had shook his hand and Ma had hugged him. They were proud of him— and he wasn't even their son.

"I want to sign up for the army with you," Leander said.

He saw the laugh that Given held inside, saw the smile that crept across his lips. "You're too young, Lee. Wait a few years."

"Pa says the war's near over. Won't last till I'm grown "

He watched Given's face soften just a mite. "If you want to earn money, you can do that at the foundry in Ironton," Given said. "The foundry makes mostly cannons these days, so you'd do your part for the war effort."

The war effort wasn't what mattered to Leander. Working in the foundry wasn't something to admire, not like being a soldier in uniform, a soldier who'd risk his life facing enemy guns. Pa had to see he was doing a manly thing. Ma, too. And Lila.

"If you did foundry work this winter," Given went on, "you could put by some money and help work your pa's land come spring."

"And have Pa and Nate scorch my ears for not working hard enough? Nate says some things are worth fighting for.

I need to prove myself, Giv. I need them to stop seeing me as a young'un."

Given opened his mouth, but closed it again without a word. Leander took his hands from the rail and put them in his pockets just like Given. The rocking of the ferry tried to throw him off his feet, but he steadied himself and hoped Given hadn't noticed.

He watched sunlight ride the river's current and wondered if Pa could manage to work the farm alone. Maybe he'd finally realize how much help Leander had been. He was on his way to join the army—like any man might do. Who could deny he was a man now?

8

JOINING UP

LEANDER STEPPED OFF THE FERRY AND STOOD ON
the ground of a new state that used to be part of Virginia.
He had never been outside Ohio before, but he reckoned
he'd need to get used to that. The army would send him to
the South—to fight. He took a deep breath and thought
about looks of pride on Pa's face. Lila's, too. He tried not to
think of Ma's worry lines.

The recruiting officer wore captain's bars and sat inside
a tent with another man. He took one look at Leander
and said, "You're too young, pup. Come back when you've
grown some."

Why was it always about size? It was tough being
scarcely taller than a fence post, tougher still to have a face
folks back home compared to a cherub in the stained-glass
church window. But that had nothing to do with being a

man. He was here to join the army, to stand side by side with other soldiers, but he kept those thoughts inside and looked down at the toes of his boots.

Given stepped forward and said, "He's with me. He might look small, but he saved his brother's life a few months ago. I seen him do it. Now he's ready to fight for his country." Given's voice had a way of making folks listen. His eyes took on a look as big as his size, and no man dared to cross him. Leander thought that if the Rebels saw that look, the whole Confederate Army would throw down their arms and surrender.

A sergeant beside the recruiting captain looked at Giv's solid-as-nail-keg arms and said, "Enlistments is way down, Cap'n. Why not let the sawbones give him a look-see?"

The captain nodded and sent Leander and Given to another tent, where a doctor's eyes took in the two of them, head to toe. He had them turn to the side and thumped each one on the back and chest. He ran his fingers along their limbs and shoulders. When his hands grasped Given's ham-like shoulders, he grunted in approval. When he stood beside Leander, he blew out his breath. "You eighteen, son?"

"I will be soon, sir." Two-and-a-half years was soon, wasn't it?

"Maybe you're not done growing yet," the doctor said

and scratched some ink across a sheet of paper. "Tell the captain I declare you fit for service."

A grin spread across Leander's face, and he couldn't wait to see the look on Pa's—and Lila's.

And Given had spoken up for him. Saving Nate's life wasn't something Leander had thought about. He'd just done it. He didn't know that Given had taken notice. He felt taller already. *Now who's a man?* he thought.

"The army isn't a lark, son," the doctor said. "Our country is at war, and you'll be expected to work hard."

"Yes, sir," Leander said and forced the grin into hiding. But deep inside he was still smiling, thinking only of what folks would say when they saw him in uniform.

9
BREAKING THE NEWS

BEFORE LEANDER CLIMBED INTO THE BACK OF THE cobbler wagon, he whispered to Given, "Don't tell your pa I joined up. Not until I tell Ma and Pa. They need to hear it from me first."

Given nodded, his lips taut and unsmiling.

During the ride home, the clattering of the lasts seemed like voices. *Foolish boy*, they seemed to say.

Maybe he should ask Given to stand beside him when he broke the news to Ma and Pa. Nate's accident had set Ma and Pa's river of words back on course. What would Leander's enlistment do? He hadn't thought of that. He didn't want to cause trouble between them. He didn't want to cause Ma more pain. But he had to face them. And he had to do it without Given. Like a man would do.

★ ★ ★

Nate was in his chair on the porch, so Leander told him first. "They let me sign up. I'm in the army." He didn't mention how Given had stepped forward to convince them.

Nate's face went slack, looking almost dead, like it had on the bank of the pond back in August. He opened his mouth to speak, but just let out his breath and shook his head.

Leander had to find some deep-down courage before he faced Ma and Pa. Now he knew why it had been hard for Nate.

He waited until supper, just as Nate had. He fidgeted the same fidgets, winced the same wince, and stopped short of tugging at his collar. Finally he breathed deep and spilled out the words, all in one breath. "I joined the army with Given today, I swore the oath of allegiance, and they read us the Articles of War."

Pa didn't bellow, and Leander suspected Nate had prepared him. Nate and Pa seemed to talk over everything.

But Ma gasped and shrieked. "No, no, no. You can't!"

Pa put his hand on Leander's shoulder and said with a grimace, "You've made a rash move, son. But you're only a boy, and we can get you out of this."

"I don't want out of it. You keep telling me I need to be a man, so let me be one."

"That's not what your pa meant, Leander." Ma used the tone she had used when Leander was five years old. "He just wanted you to work harder. We need you here, especially now that . . ." Her eyes went to Nate.

"I never work hard enough to suit Pa." Leander's voice rose. "To him, I'll always be a malingerer. Why does he need *me*?"

Ma looked at Pa. "Tell him. Tell him you need him here."

Pa cleared his throat. "Of course we do. I never meant to. . . . This is not what we want for you, son."

Leander forced his voice to stay calm. "You always tell me what you want is for me to be a man. A man keeps his word, and I swore the oath."

Ma sniffled and started to say something, but Pa shushed her with a look. Leander feared she'd clear dishes in silence just as she had all those months ago, but she dropped her head in her hands and cried. Leander wanted to hug her, to reassure her, to tell her everything would turn out for the best, but he stayed face-to-face with Pa. He squared his shoulders and stood firm.

Pa stared at him as though he'd never seen him before.

It was a far different look from the look of pride Pa'd had for Nate at that other supper.

"I have chores to do," Leander said, and strode out to the grazing patch to fetch Birdie.

★ ★ ★

After facing Ma and Pa, Leander reckoned telling Lila would be easy.

"Me and Given will leave in two weeks to be mustered in and trained," he told her, as they walked among haystacks in Pa's field.

"I know." She plucked a handful of hay from a stack and wrapped it around her fingers. "Giv told me. What did you go and do something so crazy for?"

I wanted to show you and everyone else I'm a man, he thought. But he couldn't make his mouth say the words out loud. What he said was, "Do you think Given is crazy, too? What about when Nate was going to go?"

"All men are crazy, and none of them seems to care what I think." She let the hay fly in the wind. The look she gave him wasn't the look he had hoped for. And the tone of her voice reminded him of the lasts in the cobbler wagon, making him feel shriveled down to the size of a runt pig.

47

10
FAREWELL

THE DAY BEFORE LEANDER AND GIVEN WERE TO leave for the army, sunshine sparkled on the morning's frost and decorated the crisp late-autumn day.

Their families had invited a few neighbors for a farewell dinner. Given fetched sawhorses from the barn and helped Pa lay long boards across them for a table.

Ma cooked, and Mrs. McGlade baked bread and applesauce cake. Ma thanked her and smiled, but her smile reminded Leander of the doll Lila had toted when she was a young'un, a doll whose unchanging smile was stitched on with thread.

Carrying dishes and serving food, Ma's hands were too full to dab at tears in her eyes. Leander tried to help her, but she shooed him away.

"I can't believe you're going into the army," Ruth Walsh

said, a look on her face like the one he had hoped to see on Lila's. Ruth hung near his elbow as everyone ate and filled their plates again until their bellies clamored in protest.

Ma wore that stitched-on smile and said cheery things to the guests. Likely, only Leander and Nate noticed the silence she had for Pa.

When everyone had left, Leander carried a blanket to Nate on the back porch. "It's getting cold out here," he said, tucking the blanket around Nate's useless limbs.

"I asked Pa to sit me here," Nate said. "He seems to think the sight of the pond will make me sad, but it don't."

At the foot of the hill, the setting sun reflected in orange ripples on the pond, curling and changing shape with each movement of the water.

"It keeps changing right in front of you, don't it?" Leander said. He meant the pond, but he could have been talking about other things.

They sat beside one another, as they had when they were small boys. Leander found himself remembering those other times.

"Army life won't be easy," Nate said without preamble.

"I know. Don't *you* know I ain't a young'un no more?"

Nate hesitated a moment before he spoke. "Could be I'm jealous you're going to be the soldier I planned to be, and could be I'm scared my little brother might get hisself killed."

"Truly, Nate? You're scared for me?"

"If you didn't come back, I'd miss you—for at least a week." Nate laughed and jabbed Leander lightly in the ribs. "Truth is I saw what you're made of that day you pulled me out of the pond. I don't reckon I thanked you proper for that."

"If you want to thank me, look out for Ma while I'm gone. Maybe you can get her to speak to Pa again once I leave?"

"I expect they'll make amends sooner or later."

"If she feels the need to be cross, she should be cross with *me*. I'm the one who joined up."

"She ain't going to be cross with her baby boy, especially now that you're going away."

"I ain't a baby no more."

"I know," Nate admitted with a nod. "But it's going to take time for us to think of you as a soldier."

He and Leander sat quiet as the orange waves sank into the pond. The sunset's reflection would be back over the pond again tomorrow, but Leander wouldn't be here to see it. He'd see the sunset from an army camp.

Alone in the loft, he tugged on his nightshirt. He recalled how he and Nate used to whisper across the room to each other—when Nate could still climb the ladder. Silence fell loud on his ears.

He stretched out in bed, hands clasped behind his head—wide awake. Worry about Ma, sadness at leaving home, thoughts about the army, and concern for what lay ahead left no room for sleep. Doubts crowded into bed beside him, and he tried to push them out. He had to go. He had already sworn the oath.

★ ★ ★

Next morning, Ma kissed his cheek and hugged him so long he feared he might miss his train. Pa reached out to hug him, but Leander stepped back and shook his hand—like a man would do. He shook Nate's hand, too.

He saved Lila's hug for last. She hugged him so tight he thought her imprint would be forever a part of him. And when she stepped away, she left a warm tear on his cheek.

11
IN CAMP

H EY, MAMA'S BOY!" THE DEEP VOICE taunted. "What ya got there? Did Mama send ya somethin' from home? Maybe a raggy doll to sleep with at night?" A husky, jeering laugh rang out and bounced off the trees that sheltered the camp.

Leander pretended not to hear, though all the men knew he did. Bull's voice was hard to ignore. Its bullfrog timbre had earned the man his nickname, and it carried as though the air moved aside to make way for it. That voice had tormented Leander since his first day in the Union Army. From training in Ohio, to more training at their winter encampment in Kentucky, to this new camp in Tennessee, Bull never relented.

Leander had thought the army would prove him a

man. He was sixteen now, but he was treated more like a young'un than ever. Someone always barked out orders and thundered in his ears if he didn't follow them quickly enough. He dug latrines, built fires, and marched. Every day, in cold or wet, they marched. Keeping up with the other men was tougher than farm work, and the tongue-lashings worse than anything Pa had dished out.

"I saw the mail wagon, Lee," a voice broke into his thoughts. "Package from home?"

"I think Ma sent shoes." Leander tilted back his head to see Given's face. Even when Leander straightened his back, stiffened his legs, and pulled himself up to his tallest, he scarcely reached the middle of Given McGlade's barrel chest. No man in their company was as tall as Given. "I sent tracings of my feet so's your pa could make 'em for me. I wrote Ma that the army shoes hurt my feet."

"Could be the army makes its shoes the same place it makes the hardtack we eat," Given said with a grin.

Leander found a quiet place between two trees to open his package. Tennessee had ashes, sycamores, and river birches, but some unfamiliar trees stood as tall reminders that he was far from home.

The smell of new leather made him smile as he

scrunched his feet into shoes made just for them. He had room enough to wriggle his toes, but no more. The thick-soled, army-issue brogans must have been intended for a tree, because they had near enough room for roots. Marching would be less painful now.

Ma had come through like always, even though he'd left home with little warning and no regard for how his leaving would affect her and Pa. Were they speaking yet? He knew he was to blame if they weren't.

He swallowed back a feeling of shame and stood up to admire his shoes. A gap yawned between his socks and the hem of his trousers, a gap that hadn't been there before. He was taller than he used to be, maybe even taller than Lila. He wondered if any of the men in Company D had noticed he'd grown.

Company D had been together for more than five months, and nearly every man in Mess Four had been dubbed by the others with a nickname. Twig was as thin as one, and Gator's pockmarked face looked almost reptilian. Given McGlade was simply Big'un.

If Bull had had his way, Leander would carry the weight of a nickname like Mama's Boy or Apron Strings, but Giv had stood beside him, straight and tall like a poplar, and said in his quiet yet powerful way, "His name is Leander Jordan—Jordan like the river." Most of the men called him River, a name he liked. Having grown up within spitting distance of the mighty Ohio, he felt a kinship with water.

Given had been beside Leander through all their training and drilling during winter encampment. When homesickness tried to settle into Leander, Given made him smile with a remark about the monotony of army life.

"Today's like yesterday," he said once. "We got so good at it, we'll do it again tomorrow."

Now they were close to the Georgia line, and they didn't drill much anymore. The cabins of winter had been replaced by neat rows of small tents the men carried with them and pitched at each new site.

Leander began a letter to Ma. He had to finish it before the mail wagon made ready to leave. Since they'd been in the South, the mail had been less regular, and he didn't want to miss this chance to write home.

He thanked Ma for the shoes, and said he missed her and Pa and home. He didn't write about how tough the army was or ask about spring planting. It was easier not to think about the struggle Pa might have with one son crippled and the other far from home. He was feeling enough blame for one day.

He said he hoped Nate was feeling better, but didn't mention Lila. He didn't think Ma would understand how much he missed Lila. What did Ma know about a boy's heart? No, a man's heart. Surely he was a man now, no matter who treated him like a young'un.

12

NIGHT GUARD

L EANDER STILL HADN'T FACED BATTLE, HADN'T EVEN seen the enemy. In North Georgia, Company D seemed to wage war with the Memphis and Charleston Railroad, blowing up trestles and tearing up track. Hard work, but no fighting. Their mission was to keep supplies from getting through to Rebel troops. Three nights in a row, they made huge fires of railroad ties.

The fire burned low now as Leander stood night guard. He was close enough to smell the fire's smoke, but too far to feel its warmth or hear its friendly crackle.

Standing guard did not mean *standing*. Leander hadn't stood still for a minute. He walked his stretch of ground until he reached Twig's stretch of ground, nodded to Twig, turned, and walked back the way he'd come. At the other end, he exchanged nods with a soldier from Mess Five, and headed back toward Twig.

At the beginning of his watch, his eyes saw nothing in the distance except darkness, but now he saw trees, darker black against the black night. And beyond the trees, a fingernail moon spilled a dollop of light on distant hilltops.

He was tired, but thankful for his comfortable new shoes. Each trip over the same ground showed him only the same trees, the same hills, the same moon. He had to concentrate to keep his eyelids at attention, but his mind kept drifting back to Ohio and Lila. How he'd like to be in the moonlight with her.

More than half of his two-hour watch had passed, and his feet knew every step of uneven ground, every clump of grass, every hole. Before long, he could crawl into the tent he shared with Given and let his eyelids be at ease.

He reached the spot where Twig should have been, but there was no Twig, and he didn't hear Twig's footsteps.

"Twig," he whispered into the darkness. "Twig, you there?"

No answer.

He had seen no trace of Rebels in all the months he'd been in the army, but he wasn't sure what kind of animals made their homes in this unfamiliar darkness. Had something attacked Twig?

He gripped his rifle tighter and crossed the invisible line dividing his post from Twig's. After every few steps, he stopped and listened, hearing only owls, crickets, the wind.

More paces, more listening. This time he heard something. A quiet growl. He slid a shaking finger toward the trigger of his Enfield. He gazed into the darkness, looking for the glistening eyes of a night predator. Only darkness.

He held his breath and headed toward the growl. Slowly. Quietly. The growl grew louder. And a snort hung onto the end of it. Leander nearly laughed out loud at his fear. He knew this sound. He heard it every night, lying in the tent beside Given, among the tents of other men. Snoring.

He found Twig asleep, leaning against a tree trunk.

Leander gently shook the man's shoulder. "Twig, wake up. You're on guard duty."

"What? River? Lordy, my feet were achin' like they'd been door-slammed, and I sat down. I was goin' to get right back up. I swear. Don't tell Sergeant I fell asleep. You know they can hang me for sleepin' on guard duty. You won't tell, will ya?"

Leander knew he'd fought to keep his own eyes open. Surely, Twig shouldn't die for it. "Not a word. Just keep walking." It was hard to believe Twig would actually be hanged, but Leander's silence would save Twig the kind of torment Bull dished out.

He hurried to the spot where the man from Mess Five waited.

"Where you been, soldier? You're slowin' down. Best keep up the pace, lest I tell the cap'n you're shirkin' your duty."

Leander bit back the words that came to his lips and promised to do better. He said nothing about Twig.

13
BULL'S WARNING

LEANDER FELT BULL'S EYES ON HIM AS THEY pitched tents and dug latrines. When he turned, Bull shook his head like Ma did when he tracked in mud.

Tearing up railroad tracks and stopping Southern supplies meant their own supplies didn't always make it through. It had been nearly a week since their last draw of rations, and salt pork had been gone for three days. Hunger ate at tempers, and Leander reckoned he ought to stay far away from Bull.

Supper was on the fire, and the smell of it had Leander's tongue and stomach primed for it. Word that Kettle had shot a squirrel had made its way through Mess Four like a common louse, and the men were itching for a hot meal.

The soup was hot enough to warm Leander's innards, but had no more squirrel taste than water a squirrel had dipped one paw into. Leander couldn't find a single bite of meat. Still, Kettle had managed to give the soup some flavor with seasonings he carried in tins and papers. And anything wet made the flat slabs of hardtack chewable. Leander broke off a piece and dipped it into the steaming broth as Sergeant Wallace strode over to the fire.

"Cap'n thinks the Rebs have a camp just over that hill," Wallace said, pointing to a tree-covered slope hardly more distant than the McGlade farm was from the Jordan farm back home.

Every voice except Wallace's went silent.

Leander looked up from his soup and studied the sergeant's face, as though he could read the words that came from his mouth. He'd known they were in enemy territory, but he hadn't thought of Rebs being so close. Maybe Reb lookouts watched the glimmer from the very fire that warmed him. He backed away from its light and thought about those huge fires of railroad ties. Had the enemy seen those? Had he been watched on guard duty last night?

"Likely we'll meet 'em in battle come morning," Wallace went on, "but in case they try to sneak up on us during the night, Cap'n says to sleep on our arms tonight."

They'd never been told to sleep on their arms before,

and Leander knew it didn't mean to actually tuck his Enfield under his bedroll, but he had to have it beside him and at the ready while he slept—if he could sleep. How could he sleep knowing the enemy might sneak up during the night?

As a deep blackness settled around the edges of the tent line, the firelight flickered and danced. Every crackle from its flames left Leander skittish. Every night sound might be Rebel soldiers out there in the dark. He was glad it wasn't his turn for guard duty.

The man they called Fiddle opened his worn case, raised the instrument to his shoulder, and drew the bow across its strings. He played "Home Sweet Home" and other songs that made it sound as though the fiddle were crying. Did the Rebels hear the music? Did it cause them to think of Southern homes?

Ma and Pa and Nate came to Leander's mind, but not the way they were now. In his thoughts, Nate stood and ran, Ma and Pa talked together and laughed, Ma's face had no worry lines.

When Fiddle played "Jeanie with the Light Brown Hair," Leander sang the words Lila and blond hair under his breath. That farewell hug was getting hard to remember. He leaned against an oak's solid trunk, closed his eyes, and tried to see Lila's face.

"Well, lookee that. Mama's Boy is sleeping like a baby." Leander's eyes flew open as the gravelly voice continued to taunt him. "You tryin' to dream yourself back home to your mama? She ain't gonna be able to help you tomorrow."

"Back off, Bull." Given stepped forward, blocking the light of the campfire behind him. "He's U.S. Army same as you and me, and he stood guard last night while you got a good night's rest."

Instead of backing down the way he usually did when he stood in Giv's shadow, Bull swaggered right up to him and spoke. "From what I hear, he kept Nolan from Mess Five waitin' a spell. Them short legs of his can't make a proper stride."

I'm not the one who fell asleep on night watch, Leander thought. His eyes searched out Twig's, but Twig stared down at the cup of coffee in his hands.

"If we're goin' into battle come mornin'," Bull went on, "I don't want some puny mama's boy makin' stupid mistakes that could get me killed." Spit flew from Bull's mouth as he talked.

But Giv didn't step back. "He trained same as you and me. He won't make a mistake."

"He might've trained with us, but he's the only armpit

64

shooter in the whole dang company. How can I trust my life to an armpit shooter?"

Armpit shooter! Leander jumped to his feet. If only he were big enough to make Bull take it back. But if he were bigger, he wouldn't be an "armpit shooter."

When firing, the other soldiers leaned the butts of their rifles into their shoulders, but Leander's arms were too short to steady his weapon that way. He had to tuck his under his arm when he raised it. He looked around at all the faces, but no one spoke up against Bull except Given.

"Come on, Lee, let's get our rifles cleaned," Giv said.

"You best stand over him and make sure he cleans it right," Bull called after them.

14

PREPARING FOR BATTLE

S ITTING OUTSIDE THEIR SMALL TENT, LEANDER watched Giv run his cleaning cloth down his rifle barrel with his ramrod.

Leander couldn't slow his racing pulse. "Do you think we're truly going into battle, Giv?"

"Just make sure you got that gun good and clean and ready."

"You told Bull I won't make a mistake," Leander said. "Did you mean it?"

"Mistakes can happen to anybody. But if it happens to *you*, I'm the one your folks'll blame. I helped get you into the army."

"But you tried to talk me out of it first. You said I should work at the foundry."

Given sighed. "Sometimes I wish you had listened. But I never saw you so determined before. Now clean that gun proper, and don't make me regret what I did."

"I won't, Giv. I swear." He oiled his cleaning cloth, slid it down his rifle barrel, and worked it around with the ramrod to clean its insides of every bit of soot and powder. He cleaned it twice just to be sure. There could be no mistakes.

★　★　★

Later, he crawled into the tent and shifted position a few times until his body conformed to the earth's hard lumps beneath his bedroll. His back pressed against the warmth of Giv's back, and he curled his legs to keep his feet under his skimpy blanket. Given's legs stuck out all the way to his knees.

Leander reached out and touched his rifle, ran his fingers down its cool, smooth barrel, stroked its wooden stock. "Giv, you think that we could die tomorrow?"

Given didn't answer right away, and Leander wondered if he had fallen asleep. Leander's face was so close to the side of the tent, he smelled its dampness. His eyes began to adjust to the dark and he saw a glimpse of moonlight through the canvas. He moved his foot and felt the solid stock of his gun beside him. His shoulder leaned against its barrel. Even with the new inches he had grown, the Enfield was taller than he was.

He heard Given suck in his breath before saying, "Anybody could die on any tomorrow. Your brother dang near died in that swimming hole last summer. Best not to linger on 'could-happens.' Get some sleep."

Sleep seemed more distant than the Rebel encampment on the other side of the hill. Leander let his finger brush inside the trigger guard of his Enfield. He hadn't used the rifle yet except for drilling and shooting practice, hadn't shot so much as a squirrel. Tomorrow that could change. Would he have the courage to squeeze that trigger and kill a Rebel soldier? Would the Rebel shoot first? It was hard *not* to think about a could-happen. A could-happen Giv would be blamed for.

"Hey, Giv," he began, but Given's quiet snores filled the tent. How could he sleep so peacefully?

Leander squirmed under his blanket. A clod of dirt pressed into his shoulder, but that was the least of his worries. Sleep would have been a whole heap easier for a foundry worker.

15
BATTLE

SLEEP CAME IN FITFUL SPURTS, AND LEANDER WOKE again and again, shivering with a chill his blanket couldn't ease. The clod of dirt under his bedroll jabbed him no matter what position he curled into.

Snippets of dreams spilled into his brain every time he nodded off. *Rebels were shooting.* He startled awake. *Ma was crying.* He thrashed back into wakefulness. *He swam in the pond with Lila, and Nate tugged on his foot.*

"Stop it, Nate!"

"Quiet," came a harsh whisper from Gator. "It's time to fall in."

"What?" His eyes flew open. Had he slept through reveille?

"Quiet!" Gator's head leaned into the tent, his tone harsher this time. "Cap'n wants us ready to march."

69

Given was already rolling his bedroll and striking the tent before Leander had completely crawled out of it.

Pushing his feet into his new shoes, he rubbed his eyes and strained to see the rushed movements that he heard in the dark around him. Given had stowed the tent and stood in the muster line between Twig and Gator. Leander rolled his bedroll and hurried to join them.

When all the men were in line, Sergeant Wallace began the orders for loading their rifles, but in a loud whisper instead of his usual crisp bark.

"I didn't think we were supposed to load until we were ready to fire," Leander whispered to Given.

"Quiet in the ranks!" Wallace demanded.

Leander ripped open the paper cartridge with his teeth and dumped the powder down the barrel of his Enfield. He wadded the paper and, using his ramrod, lightly tamped in both paper and ball. When he rested the rifle on his shoulder, everyone else's was already in place.

"The Rebs ain't stirring yet," Wallace continued in his loud whisper. "We're going to give them one hell of a reveille. Fall in! Prepare to march!"

Leander fell into step next to Given, tightly gripping his Enfield, and headed toward the hill barely visible in the dark, the hill where the Rebels were camped. It was more distant than it had seemed the night before. They had to advance into a gully and cross a creek. The creek was shallow enough to cross easily, but the bank on the far side was slippery with mud—and steep. They broke formation and used their hands to climb it.

Leander's right hand gripped his Enfield and his left grabbed at clumps of grass to pull himself up. Most of the men scaled the bank with little effort, but Leander's shoes slid and pitched him forward. His rifle barrel kept him from planting his face in the mud, and he looked around to see if anyone had seen his fall. Bull didn't need another reason to torment him.

But the others had already disappeared into the darkness.

He quickly retrieved his weapon, used the butt of it to push himself back to his feet, and scrambled to keep going.

Once up the bank, he ran to catch up with the men and fell into position beside Given. They marched across a field of knee-high grass toward the hill, which stood as a large lump against the eastern sky. The sun pinkened the outline of that lump where the enemy lay. Under a still-dark sky, Leander struggled to keep up with the long strides of the others.

Crack! Crack! Crack! Rifle fire came from the hill, sending small explosions of soil and grass into the air in front of them.

"Prepare to return fire!" came the distant order.

"Prepare to return fire!" Sergeant Wallace repeated.

Leander fell to one knee beside Given and the rest of the front line. Hammers clicked into half-cocked position. He seated a cap opposite the hammer of his rifle and tucked the end of its stock under his right armpit. He stretched out his left arm and steadied the barrel. A sidewise look showed him the steadfast set of Given's jaw.

Crack! Crack! Puffs of dark-gray smoke rose from a point halfway up the hillside. Leander aimed his rifle at a puff of smoke and waited for the order.

"Fire!" came the distant call.

"Fire!" Wallace repeated.

Rifles sounded along the firing line, and the acrid, rotten-egg smell of gun smoke bit the air. Leander slid his finger into the trigger guard and squeezed the trigger.

A bright flash! A loud *BAM!* Pain! The black sky swooped down and swallowed him whole.

16

INJURED

THE DARK SQUEEZED LEANDER. HE GASPED AND struggled for air. When he finally got a breath, the air smelled charred, and smoke seared his throat. Waves of pain surged through him.

He felt himself being lifted. *I died and the Lord is carrying me to Heaven.*

But it wasn't the Lord. His eyes blinked open and he saw grass and shoes and trouser legs. He was certain the solid object pressing into his belly was the broad shoulder of Given McGlade, and he was being carried just as Nate had been last summer.

With every step Given took, Leander was jostled. White-hot pain gushed into every inch of him. He closed his eyes and tried to will it away. But each step brought it back, sharpened it. A cry escaped from deep inside him, but by the time the sound made its way to his lips, it had left a trail of pain from his lungs to his throat to his mouth.

When he opened his eyes, he saw red drops falling, raining beneath him to stain the legs of Giv's uniform. Given was bleeding!

Just before Leander's eyes closed again, he realized it wasn't Given's blood.

★ ★ ★

Ma waved a tied rag of herbs under Leander's nose. Not like any herbs he'd ever smelled before. They were sharp and pungent and burned his nose. He tried to turn his head away from the rag, but he couldn't move. Not his head. Not his arms. Not his legs.

He couldn't breathe. He was underwater, pinned beneath the rock shelf in their pond. He tried to swim out from under it, but that sharp smell pulled him deep into the blackness. He gasped for air that wasn't there.

A hand reached out to him and he felt a tug on his right arm. The tug turned into hard pulling, and Leander tried to let himself be rescued, but he was stuck fast.

"I'm dying," he thought. His eyes labored to open, and a hand touched his forehead. When he forced open his eyes, he saw concern in Lila's blue ones. She wiped pond water from his face with a towel. She stroked his cheek with her hand, and he leaned his face into her touch.

Nate came up behind Lila and pulled on Leander's arm. "Get up! Get up!" he shouted. "You have to be a man."

"He's a young'un," Lila said, "just a young'un."

A wavering light behind them hurt Leander's eyes. He looked away from it and down Nate's legs. Nate was standing! His legs were whole again, but Nate seemed angry. He kept pulling on his brother's arm.

"Stop it, Nate. That hurts."

But Nate kept pulling.

★ ★ ★

"Lee." A quiet voice reached across Nate and Lila and the blackness. "Lee, wake up."

Leander opened his eyes, but light stabbed into them, forcing them closed again. They didn't hurt as much when they were closed.

"I'm here, Lee," the voice said again.

He opened his eyes once more and saw the blue of Lila's.

"It's me, Lee. I'm here." The voice was deep. Not Lila's. He struggled against the flickering light. The blue eyes looked out from a face rough with whiskers. Given.

Leander tried to talk, but his throat felt burnt, and words stung its soreness. This time, in spite of the pain, he forced his eyes to stay open. The light came from stubby candles stuck onto detached bayonets and made shadows on canvas above him. The shadows grew and shrank and grew again, changing shape and looming like specters.

Leander strained to speak around the pain in his throat. "Am I truly alive, Giv?"

A ragged laugh. "You sure are," Given said. The side of Giv's face was bloody, burnt, and raw, and one eye was red and swollen almost shut.

"I saw Nate and Lila."

"It was just a dream. All you saw was the army surgeon. You need to rest now."

The surgeon! Leander groped for a memory. He knew he had fired on the enemy. He must have been shot by a Rebel. Clearly, Given had been wounded, too. But Leander couldn't recall the battle, only the pain and the blackness.

"Don't leave, Giv." He struggled against his painful throat. "Stay with me." He tried to grab Giv's sleeve, but he couldn't. His hand wouldn't reach out.

Leander fought the pain to raise his head. He looked past his shirtless chest, where bloody bandages covered his right side—and a small lump at Leander's shoulder.

No arm. Only a lump.

17

BLAME

"**M**Y ARM, GIV! WHERE'S MY ARM?" TEARS filled Leander's eyes, and he tasted salt. The salt burned his aching throat.

No! This wasn't real. It had to be another dream. He had to be at home, safe in his own bed. Ma and Pa had to be close by. And Lila. He had to hear Lila's voice.

But the voice he heard belonged to Lila's brother. Given's voice was calm. "They had to take it, Lee. It was shredded like a fox-caught chicken. It wouldn't do you no good no more. Your whole side got quite a lick. And they tell me you breathed in a mess of smoke and fire."

"Dang Rebels tried to kill me, Giv. They got you, too."

Given reached up to his face, but stopped short of touching the place on his bloody cheek where the skin was gone. His look was like Pa's when he'd stood over

Nate and told him he was going to be fine. Giv wasn't telling him everything.

"Was the battle a bloody one, Giv? Were many killed?"

"Wasn't no battle. Just a few Reb skirmishers, tricking us into believing the whole army was out there, probably trying to slow us down while the Rebel army skedaddled."

"But they shot at us. I remember the shooting. They shot me!" He tried to reach out to Given—before he remembered his hand wasn't there anymore. "Look at you, Giv. You're bloodied, too."

Given chewed his bottom lip. Leander reached out his only hand, a hand with a burn that hurt as it brushed Given's sleeve. He was almost glad for the pain, a reminder he still had *that* hand.

"What happened, Giv? Tell me."

"The skirmishers fired a few shots at us," Given finally said, "but they didn't shoot you. Your gun blew up on ya."

"Blew up? But how?"

"Wondered that myself, so I went back out and found it whilst the surgeon was doctoring you. The muzzle was plugged with mud, so's when you fired, it blew up. Was right beside you and caught my share of it."

"But who . . . ? How . . . ? I cleaned it good, Giv. I swear. And I had it with me the whole time. How could . . . ?"

A memory raced through Leander's mind. He remembered crossing the shallow creek and clambering up the other side in the mud, falling with his rifle, and hoisting himself back up before anyone noticed. That must have been when it happened.

He had caused his gun to explode. *He* was to blame for the loss of his arm. And he'd wounded Given, too.

★　★　★

Every movement added to the pain in Leander's side and shoulder, so he lay still.

The smoke had taken a toll on his eyes and it felt better to keep them closed. There was nothing to see anyway, except the canvas of the surgeon's tent. But he heard the sounds of camp being made, tent stakes being pounded, footsteps, voices. Army life went on without him while he lay on a cot, alone and one-armed. There were no other cots because no one else had been injured. There hadn't been a battle. Leander wasn't a casualty of war. He was a casualty of carelessness. He had dishonored his uniform, Sergeant Wallace, the captain, and all the way up to General Schofield and President Lincoln.

He heard the sound of the tent flap and felt a presence. He struggled to open his eyes, but the face above him was just a silhouette against the canvas. He closed them again.

"You going to be all right, River?" a voice asked. Twig.

Leander didn't answer. He didn't know the answer. Death came often to a surgeon's tent.

"I'm sorry you got hurt," Twig said. "You kept up with the rest of us, no matter what anybody says." Twig's voice dropped to a whisper. "I appreciate you not lettin' on that I fell asleep on guard duty. You're a loyal man."

The tent flap opened again, and an army steward came inside. The man asked Leander if he needed anything.

Leander shook his head. His throat hurt too much to talk.

"I was just leavin'," Twig said to the steward. "Hope you heal up right quick," he told Leander.

"You sure I can't get you something?" the steward asked as the tent flap fell closed behind Twig. "Drink of water, maybe?"

Leander nodded. Water might ease his scorched throat.

The steward filled a dipper from the water pail and gently raised Leander's head to reach it. "Drink slow," he instructed. "It won't hurt so much that way."

But every swallow hurt like breathing fire. Leander drank the dipper dry anyway.

When the steward laid Leander's head back on the cot, he closed his eyes and tried to sleep, but sleep wouldn't come. He had lost his right arm. What good would he be to anyone? Twig said he was "a loyal man." Someone finally called him a *man*. But what difference would that make now?

He thought of home. Of Ma and Pa and Nate and Lila. Would he survive to go back home to them? And what would they say if he did? Would Ma tell Pa, *I told you so?* Would Pa's face look ashamed? Would Nate say, *You still got some growing up to do, little brother?* And Lila? What would Lila say?

18

LETTERS FROM HOME

LEANDER SLEPT FITFULLY, PAIN ROUSING HIM INTO wakefulness over and over. His throat ached and felt parched, but the worst pain came from the hand, wrist, and arm that weren't there anymore. And his right palm itched! How could that be?

Before he tried again to find sleep, he listened to the sounds outside the tent. He reckoned it must be near sunup for all the activity going on in the camp.

★ ★ ★

"The mail wagon came, Lee," Given said, entering the surgeon's tent. "Letter from your ma. One from Lila, too."

"My eyes are burnin' bad, Giv. Can you read 'em to me? I got no secrets from you."

Ma's letter told about spring back home, and her words made Leander ache for the tickle of new grass under his

82

bare feet, the sight of young sprouts shooting up from furrowed fields, and a meadowlark's song from a fencepost between their yard and Lila's. Next month, the jewelweed would bloom. If he were home, Ma could make an ointment from jewelweed to ease his pain. But no ointment would give him back his arm.

Lila's letter said she hoped he and Given had killed the whole dang Confederate Army and would come home soon. She said she missed him and Given.

Leander sighed.

"Doc Marting offered Nate a job," Given continued, reading from Lila's letter. "He's going to teach him to make medicines and work in his office."

"Nate'll like that," Leander said.

"He'll surely like bein' able to earn some money. That brother of yours wants to have enough to take care of my sister."

"Lila?"

"Only sister I got."

"Why does she need Nate to take care of her?"

"That gun exploding blow a hole in your brain or something? You know them two are gonna get married someday."

"Nate and Lila?" Saying their names together didn't sound right. Given had to be wrong. Lila was *his* girl.

Given went on. "Only reason Nate wanted to join the army was to earn enough money so's he could afford to marry Lila."

That couldn't be right. What had Nate said? *Some things are worth fighting for.* Was Lila what he'd wanted to fight for? *Leander's* Lila? Leander had planned on marrying her since he and Lila were young sprouts—though he had never spoken of it to her.

"What makes you think she wants to marry Nate?"

"You daft? Lila's been smitten with Nate since she was a young'un. I know. I lived in the same house with her all those growin'-up years. Nate was always sunup and sundown with Lila."

Without meaning to, Leander let out a loud sigh. Had he been wrong in thinking Lila wanted them to marry as much as he did?

"You and Lila was close, Lee," Giv said. "You had to know how she felt about your brother, right? Didn't she let on to ya?"

Leander thought about Lila's letter. She hadn't said she missed *him*. She'd said she missed *them*—him and Given. Her letters never spoke of love or a future with him. He tried to remember back, tried to picture Lila's eyes and read the secrets behind them, tried to remember which things had brought a grin to her face. Could he have been so wrong about her feelings?

"We were close, sure enough," was all Leander said. "Do me a favor, Giv. Don't write 'em what happened with my gun. Let me do that my ownself."

"You can tell 'em when you get home."

"Get home?"

"The men are already breaking camp. We move out in less than an hour."

That explained the clatter Leander had heard before sunup. He'd been listening to those sounds for months now, but they sounded different when he wasn't part of it. "What about me, Giv? What'll happen to me?"

"That's what I was trying to tell ya. They're sending ya home."

Home. "They're sending me home? How? When?"

"Don't know the how, but right soon, I reckon."

"What if they put me on a train, Giv? I can't go home by train. We tore up all them tracks."

19

AMBULANCE

S UNLIGHT SHIMMERED THROUGH THE OPENING IN the back of the ambulance wagon, making a golden path on the hay at Leander's feet. But the hay that enveloped him did nothing to ease the jostling of the wagon. The bumpy road kept him mindful of the pain from his lost arm, and the constant jarring rattled his head so hard he nearly feared he'd lose that, too.

The ambulance driver said he had to heal before he went home. He was still in Southern territory. Where were they taking him to heal? And what good would healing do? It wouldn't give him back his arm.

Every time he closed his eyes to escape into sleep, the wagon hit a rock, stick, or hole and jolted his eyes open again.

The wagon wasn't the only thing that kept him from

sleep. He felt betrayed. But who had betrayed him?

He remembered sitting with Lila on the bank of the Ohio, watching the wind tug at strands of her hair. She'd peppered him with questions, but all he'd thought about was how much he'd like to hold her and kiss her. He'd scarcely listened. Now he tried to recall her questions, and the recollection jolted him more than the bumpy road. *Do you think Nate will go to the barn-raising in Coal Grove? Does Nate like blackberry pie?*

How had Leander not seen it? Lila loved Nate, and Nate loved her. Leander hadn't seen what he hadn't wanted to. His betrayer was the same one who had cost him his arm.

★ ★ ★

The wagon stopped twice, and a steward came inside to spoon cold broth into Leander's mouth. The man was gentle, but the broth was tasteless with lumps of fat that clung to his teeth and tongue.

He heard a call to the horses and the jolting ride began again. The wagon bumped his head from side to side until it ached, and a chill seeped through his clothes. He couldn't get warm. He wriggled his body deeper into the hay, but still he shivered.

Dreams crept in. *He had two hands and threw railroad ties into the fire. Flames shot up higher and higher, until sweat soaked his clothes from the heat.* He woke up and pushed away the hay. The sweat was real and the wagon wouldn't stop bumping.

More dreams. *The train hurtled down the track, faster and faster, toward the trestle that Company D had blown up. He was falling, falling. He reached out to grab hold of something, but his arms were gone.*

When he woke, the opening at the rear of the ambulance showed only darkness, but the bumping and jolting continued. Every bump reminded him that something was missing, and Leander wondered which loss caused him more misery: his arm or Lila?

Cru-unch! The ambulance wagon bumped over something big, maybe a log, and threw Leander against a supply box. The edge of the box stabbed new pain into the stump at his shoulder. He cried out, but no one seemed to hear him. He gritted his teeth. Could a person die from pain? Maybe dying would be merciful.

It was still dark when the jostling stopped, but flickers of light showed through the canvas wagon cover. Two men came to the back of the wagon with a stretcher.

"Don't put me on a train," Leander told them. "You can't let anyone on a train. The tracks are tore up."

"You see a train?" one man said to the other.

"He's feverish," the second man said, touching Leander's face. "And he's bleeding through his bandage." To Leander, he said, "This is a hospital. In Rome, Georgia."

The men lifted Leander onto the stretcher and carried him up steps into a building.

Pretty fancy for a hospital, Leander thought. Most army field hospitals were tent cities, but this was like a real house—a huge one—with a staircase, curtains, and candles flickering inside glass chimneys.

The men carried him past the staircase, and as he craned his neck he saw that the stairs twisted and climbed up three more levels. He had never seen a place this big, not even in Ironton. If this was a Southern hospital, Leander had misjudged the enemy.

He was truly impressed—for half a minute. When the stretcher-bearers carried him into a room and he took his first deep breath inside the hospital, he was greeted by the stench of vomit, urine, human waste—and death.

20

PAUL

GARDENS OF FLOWERS ON THE ROOM'S wallpaper seemed out of place with the stench. And sounds of suffering came from patients on more than a dozen cots. Leander wanted to cover his ears and hold his nose, but even *two* hands couldn't have done that.

The stretcher-bearers lifted him from the stretcher onto a cot. He tried to ignore the pain that stabbed through him as they moved him, but a groan shot from his lips and was swallowed up by the moans around him.

"Cain't ya be more keerful?" A boy's scolding voice broke through the sounds.

The men mumbled what sounded like an apology, as they headed for the door and disappeared.

The boy hastened to Leander's cot. "Dadblam stretcher-toters!" he said. "Ya's bleedin' and needful of a new bandage.

Ya hurtin' considerable?" The boy's uniform was Union, but he sure sounded Southern.

Leander nodded. "Considerable," he said.

The boy began to unwind the bloody bandage from Leander's shoulder. "I ain't goin' hurt ya none," he assured. His tone was gentle—and he didn't sound more than ten years old. His voice hadn't even changed yet.

Leander watched as the boy worked, packing lint into the bloody place where his arm had been. His movements were careful, but not slow. He wrapped a new bandage around the stump and tucked it into itself to hold it in place.

The boy's face was freckled, his hair the color of Ma's copper wash pot. He looked even younger than Leander. If he were infantry, surely he was an armpit shooter like Leander. A boy like that wouldn't stand a chance around a man like Bull.

"Ya's fever-y," the boy said, holding a cloth to Leander's forehead. "I'll fetch water. Ya needs medicine, but Doc's gone till mornin'. I'm Paul Settles."

"Leander Jordan," Leander said. "Jordan, like the river."

Paul brought a water bucket and filled a dipper. He put it to Leander's lips.

Leander took water into his mouth and held it there.

He knew that swallowing would awaken the pain in his throat.

Paul's eyes coaxed. "Go ahead on now," he said.

With one gulp, Leander swallowed. And with Paul's persistence, he drained the dipper dry.

"You a hospital steward?" Leander asked.

"No, but they been shorthanded here. I was brung in with my unit when we all come up sick from pizened water. I shook off the lowlies right fast, and reckoned I'd help look after t'others. As long as I help, they's lettin' me stay. This here's my pap." Paul gestured toward a man on the next cot. The man's closed eyes sat deep in dark hollows, his cheeks redder than Paul's hair.

"Where you from?" Leander asked.

"Virginny. I mean, West Virginny. We's our own state now."

"I know about Virginia being split in two. I joined the army in West Virginia." Leander couldn't seem to stop talking.

"Git ya some rest now," Paul said. "Ya needs ta git well enough ta go home."

The thought of home brought Leander a new kind of pain.

The boy moved to his father's cot and murmured

soothing words to the man, words Leander couldn't make out. If the man understood, it didn't show.

Paul looked back at Leander. "If'n ya needs anythin', jist speak right on up. I'll be here with Pap."

"How old are you?" The words had formed in Leander's head and he hadn't meant to say them out loud, but there they were.

"Fifteen," Paul said, in a tone that dared Leander to dispute it.

Leander dared. "Ain't."

"Am."

"Ain't neither."

The boy stiffened and gave Leander a hard stare. "Nigh on sixteen, but what you know? Ya cain't be more'n twelve yourself."

Leander sat up to defend himself, but his head felt heavy and he fell back with a groan.

Paul's anger disappeared like a snuffed flame. "Ya need more water? Somethin' to eat? Anythin'?"

Leander closed his eyes. Paul couldn't give him the *anything* he wanted.

21

FEVER

*L*ILA HELD A COOL CLOTH TO LEANDER'S FOREHEAD AND *brushed his cheek with her fingertips. Her gentle voice eased its way through his pain.*

He reached up and held her hand between his own—both of them! He had two hands! He was whole again and home with Lila.

He struggled to speak, but she pressed her finger to his lips to quiet him. He kissed the tip of her finger and she whispered his name.

"Leander," a voice said, "Leander, drink this." He tasted tin and felt the slosh of water against his lips. He drank, but the water tasted bitter. The word "pizened" floated into his mind and he spat out what he hadn't swallowed.

"Hey!" the voice shouted, but quickly resumed its calmness. "Drink this. Doctor says it'll make ya well."

He looked up into the green eyes of Paul Settles and saw the spittle that dotted Paul's cheek. "Ya been fever-y all night," Paul said. "Ya needs ta take your medicine."

Leander's head was swimming, and he seemed to emerge from underwater. Lila was the dream. The nightmare was real. His eyes took in the stump at his shoulder for confirmation.

"Take your medicine." Paul used his gentle voice even though Leander had just spat at him.

Leander drank the whole bitter cup, and noticed that his throat didn't feel as burnt as before. When he shivered, Paul fetched him a blanket. When he kicked off the blanket in a fit of fever, Paul retrieved it from the floor and folded it at the foot of the cot until the next shiver took hold.

Leander watched as Paul bathed his father's face. The boy took such care. It reminded him of the way Ma had tended Nate. Leander hadn't helped her with that, and he'd resented her impatience with *him*. His mind flitted back to seeing Ma cook and clean along with caring for Nate. Never a moment's rest. Maybe she'd had good reason for impatience.

Leander shook off the heavy feeling that filled his

chest. "You don't look like him," he told Paul. "You must look like your ma."

"That's what Pap says. I never knew her. She drew her last breath same day I drew my first."

"Sorry."

"It's life's way, ain't it? Pap said her skin was fair like mine, the kind ta git red as a ripe apple in the sun. And she had freckles, too. Shucks, look at me, babblin' on and on. Ya needs ta git your rest."

"Is your father better today?"

Paul shook his head and said quietly, "Sometimes life's way ain't easy."

22
BATTLE NEWS

UNDER THE CARE OF AN ARMY SURGEON— and Paul Settles—Leander's fever abated by the third morning. His night had been rough, constant noises waking him from sweet dreams of Lila. Loud whispered voices. Metal scraping. Hurried footsteps. Now and then, a shriek of pain.

When flickering candlelight gave way to daylight, he woke again, drenched in sweat, his hair sticking to his neck and forehead, his mind trying to cling to remnants of a dream.

He leaned on his lone elbow and saw the results of the night's sounds. New makeshift cots had been constructed, and the groans and wails had multiplied. Every cot was occupied, and men lay on the floor. Paul bustled from man to man, dipping water, giving medicine, and changing bandages.

Through the noise, Leander heard men talking on cots close by. They had survived a battle at a place called New Hope Church, and they bemoaned a large number of losses. Leander heard the name *Schofield*.

"Are you with General Schofield's men?" he asked.

"We are," one man replied.

"You know Given McGlade? Big fellow? Tree-size big? From Company D?"

"Don't know the name."

"But there were casualties?"

"Son, that field was mighty bloody when they hauled us off it. And bodies were everywhere."

Another man called for water, and Paul hustled to his side. The strain of lifting the heavy water bucket showed on Paul's face as he hefted it to the cot, but the tautness vanished as he greeted the man with a soothing look and a dipper of water.

If he's fifteen, I'm Given McGlade's twin, Leander thought.

Given. Had Given been in that battle at New Hope Church? Was he among those bodies the man spoke of?

Just lying there was more than Leander could bear. He wanted to do something. He couldn't be in a battle, couldn't help Given, but he could help Paul take care of Schofield's men. Even with one arm, lifting the heavy water bucket should be easy. The burn on his hand was nearly healed.

He sat on the edge of the cot and eased his feet into his shoes. He could barely feel them. He tried to stand, but his legs refused to support his weight. He had to sit back down in a hurry.

"What you tryin' ta do?" Paul was beside him in a blink.

"I thought I'd give you a hand," Leander said, "but my limbs seem to have lost their starch."

"Ya been so all-fired sick, I don't rightly know why ya's still breathin'," Paul said. "Jist stay where ya are till the doc says otherwise. If ya's needin' a drink of water, a bite ta eat, I'll fetch it. I'll write a letter home fer ya—if ya spell it out. I know my alphabet, but I cain't spell worth shucks."

Leander wasn't ready to write a letter home. What would he say? *Happy to hear Nate's got a job so he can afford to marry Lila. With one arm, I am a more useless son than I was before.*

"Maybe just a drink of water," he said to Paul. "And please tell me if they bring in a patient named McGlade."

23

THE RIVER'S PROMISE

S UMMER HADN'T ARRIVED ON THE CALENDAR, BUT
it sent its weather on ahead. The heat became so oppressive
Leander half-expected the wallpaper flowers to wilt.

In spite of the heat, he felt stronger every day. With
Paul's help, he was able to stand.

"That's a good beginnin'," Paul said. "You'll be fine as a
flea's eyelash afore ya know it."

"Can you take me to the window?" Leander asked. "If
I can't *go* outside, I'd sure like to look at it—and catch a
smell of it."

He draped his arm across Paul's shoulder and felt the
boy wince beneath his weight. Together they hobbled
across the floor, being mindful not to step too close to the
wounded men lying there.

Leander leaned on the wooden windowsill, taking his

weight off Paul. The window, at the rear of the house, overlooked fields of brown stalks with a scattering of white flowers. In the distance beyond the fields, a dark, shadowy line stretched the whole width of the fields and beyond, a familiar line that reminded Leander of a dark ribbon on another horizon. In his bones, he knew it was a river, and thoughts of the Ohio seeped into his mind. Already, he seemed to feel cool river air. When he was stronger, he'd have to walk through those fields and let the river breezes stroke his face.

★ ★ ★

Leander sat beside Lila on the grassy hill overlooking the riverbank. Morning sunlight shone on the water, its gleaming ripples reaching upstream and down.

A deep-throated whistle sounded in the distance, and they watched for the steamboat to round the bend. Leander's hand shielded his eyes against the sun, as Lila gripped his other hand in anticipation.

His dreams were always like that. He had two hands, and Lila was there. But it had felt real. Perhaps it had been as much memory as dream. He knew that spot, had often watched a riverboat steam by, leaving its smoke trail lingering above its wake.

But the dream was over. There was no steamboat, no

river, no Lila. That was a different life. His life now was on a cot in the rank air of a hot room—with a stump where his arm used to be.

The river beyond the brown fields seemed to call to him, seemed to promise him something. No, it wasn't Lila and the past he'd dreamed of, but that promise made it possible for Leander to get through painful days of lying in his own filth and smelling the stench of others.

Moans and cries from around him were almost as unbearable as the silence that intruded when the noises stopped. Quiet sometimes triggered a visit from the burial detail, who wordlessly hauled out a lifeless body.

Leander made his own promise. One day, he would leave this place on his own two feet.

24
THE COOSA

EACH DAY, LEANDER FELT STRONGER. THE USELESS stump at his shoulder was almost healed. He could feed himself with his left hand and rarely needed Paul's help. He could get up and walk to the privy—though it took three times longer to drop his trousers and open his drawers with only one hand. The effort of going to and from took all his strength. He always paused before he went back inside, paused to catch his breath and look toward the river before he trudged to the wallpapered room, where the smells were worse than any privy.

He had become accustomed to the moans, a constant hum in the background, but there was no getting used to the unbearable Georgia heat. When rain pattered against the windowpane and splashed into tiny puddles on the floor, a breeze sometimes found its way to Leander's cot, but mostly the rain just made the air thicker and the heat more oppressive.

He felt capable of helping Paul tend the patients now, but Paul shooed him away.

"Ya's s'posed ta be a-mendin' your arm. When ya's well enough, they'll send ya home."

Home. The word filled Leander with dread. He wasn't ready to see Lila and Nate together, not ready to tell Ma and Pa that being careless had cost him his arm. If Pa and Nate had thought he wasn't man enough to work the fields with two arms, what would they think now?

"Ya want me ta write a letter home fer ya?" Paul asked.

Leander shook his head. He wasn't ready yet. How could he prepare Ma and Pa for a one-armed son? And Lila? Did she even want to hear from him?

"Ya ought ta write to 'em," Paul said. "They'll send ya home soon as ya's strong enough. Me? I'm strong enough to send back ta the fightin'. Onliest reason they let me stay's on account of I help take care of the patients. If'n I go back, who'll look after Pap?"

Paul was a more caring son than Leander had been, and Leander vowed to do better. But all the "looking after" hadn't seemed to help Paul's father. The sound of the man's broken breathing reached through the night and into Leander's sleep.

★ ★ ★

Since stubborn Paul refused his help, Leander eased from the room, past the winding staircase, and through the open door at the rear of the house. He sat on the peeling paint of a porch step and watched a soldier fill water buckets from a well. Leander nodded a hello and the soldier grunted one back.

"That a river beyond that field?" Leander asked.

"The Coosa," answered the soldier.

"Coosa," Leander repeated. He had never heard of it, but he liked the sound. Even the name felt like a breeze.

He walked to the field that stood between him and the river. The white specks on the plants weren't flowers at all, but cotton. It was the first cotton field he had ever seen.

Easing along the field, he found an opening, a path through the plants. He looked back at the house, at the soldier filling water buckets. He thought of the hospital's smell and knew he had to follow the path, if only to find clean river air to breathe. He could do it. He was strong enough now.

The path led him to the riverbank, where the flow of

water meandered a mere stone's throw away. The current didn't look swift, and the temptation to cool himself took hold.

An aged sycamore stood guard beside the water's edge, where the river had left obvious signs of its comings and goings. The sycamore's naked roots reached out over the water and made a perfect place for Leander to grab hold, in case the current was too swift for a one-armed soldier.

He looked back toward the house again. Above the tops of the cotton plants, he could barely see its roof. His one hand fumbled with buttons as he stripped down to his drawers and tucked his clothes and shoes in the crook of a sycamore branch. He waded into the water, holding fast to a strong sycamore root. The cold water startled him at first, but he eased deeper, letting the water slither up his legs to his waist.

With his next step, the river bottom disappeared in a sudden drop-off, and before he could find his balance, a fierce tug pulled the root from his grasp. He struggled to keep his face above water, as he felt his body being pulled by the current.

25
SPYING

L EANDER GULPED WATER AND SPAT IT OUT.
I'm not going to drown, he told himself. He had been a good
swimmer, back when he was stronger. He had to make his
body do it.

He flipped over to his stomach and, using his one arm,
he swam back toward the sycamore. The river pulled hard,
but Leander pulled harder. He reached out for a sturdy
root, and caught hold.

With a tight grip on the root, he let his breathing
slow to its usual pace before testing the current. Most of
its strength ran well below the surface, past the drop-off
and along the river bottom. He pulled himself back to
waist-deep water. Settling his feet in squishy river mud, he
chided himself for having been scared. Feeling safe again
and holding tight to the root, Leander ducked down to his

shoulders and let water flow around him, soaking him in memories of the pig-shaped pond and home.

He plucked his feet from the river bottom and stretched out in the water's grasp. He leaned his head back and let the river surround him with soothing sounds and nestle him in its waters. Homesickness seemed to ooze from his pores and float downriver.

When he reckoned it was close to mess time, he ducked his head beneath the surface one last time. One last time he lifted it from the water and shook it like a dog come in from the rain.

As he steadied his feet to stand up in the spongy mud, he saw Paul Settles edge around the rows of cotton plants.

Leander didn't call out, waiting for the boy to get close enough to hear him over the swooshing sound of the Coosa. He noticed the furtive way Paul's eyes looked at the field, back toward the house, up and downriver, and back to the house again. Leander stayed quiet, wanting to see what Paul was up to.

Without turning loose his handhold, Leander dove deeper to drift beneath the roots of the sycamore. He emerged with roots all around him like a cage, hiding him from Paul's view. He felt like an army scout, keeping watch on the enemy. Not that he suspected Paul was a Reb—

even with his Southern talk—but the boy had obviously sneaked away from his duties.

Paul's eyes darted around again and even looked right at the sycamore roots. Leander ducked his chin and mouth below the surface, so the dark shadows between roots and water would keep him from being spotted.

The boy stood on the riverbank and looked out across its shimmering surface. Was he searching for something?

Leander stayed low in the water, letting the river slosh against his lips and brush past his ears. He dipped slightly with the movement of the water to stay at the level where he could hide, yet breathe through his nose while he watched.

After another sweeping gaze, Paul shucked off his shoes and socks, and dipped a toe in the water. One more look, and he stripped off his uniform shirt and trousers, and stood on the riverbank in his drawers—long-sleeved Union drawers just like Leander's.

But the boy's slight body didn't fill out the drawers the way Leander's did, and beneath the fabric, parts of it weren't at all slight.

Paul waded into shallow water at the river's edge, moving deeper to let the water cover his legs and middle. Leander watched him pull his arms from the sleeves of his drawers and commence to wash himself in the Coosa.

If Leander's mouth hadn't been still below the surface, he'd have let go a gasp that not only Paul would have heard, but likely all the patients up at the hospital.

Paul wasn't a Paul! He was a *she!*

26

THE GIRL

NOT ONLY WAS PAUL A GIRL, BUT RIGHT NOW he—rather, she—was a near-naked one. Leander had never seen a naked girl before, except maybe in his dreams about Lila. His eyes eased along her freckled shoulders to the smooth roundness of her breasts. He knew it was wrong to crouch here, hiding under the roots, watching her like a common Peeping Tom, but his eyes refused to look away.

When Paul finished washing himself—herself!—she slipped her arms back into the sleeves of her drawers. She looked toward the house again before she commenced swimming. She was a good swimmer—for a girl. Probably not as good as the two-armed Leander had been, but a good swimmer all the same.

She swam out into the river, and just when Leander

reckoned she might go clean to the other side, she turned around and swam back. Once she was close to the riverbank, she lay on her back and floated.

Leander knew how that felt. He had done it just moments ago. He knew it was a way to slough off whatever ails a body, a way to be comforted in the bosom of the water.

But the current carried the girl's body closer and closer to Leander's hiding place. He edged back as far as the roots would allow, fearful she'd discover him.

When the girl was mere yards away, she stood up on the river bottom and climbed up the bank. Leander would have let out a breath of relief had he not worried she would hear it. He watched as she slipped her uniform over now-wet drawers.

When the girl disappeared down the path through the cotton field, Leander swam out from his hiding place and waded ashore. He tugged on his uniform, but it didn't slide easily over his wet drawers. His single hand fumbled and yanked. When he finally slid his feet into his socks and shoes, the sun was already painting a bright orange glow along the horizon, and the sycamore's shadow reached farther than its height.

Leander hurried along the dark path, his breath coming

in gasps. This was the most his body had done since that day his gun blew up. He reached the back porch to find guards standing twilight watch.

"Hold up," a guard ordered, and leveled his rifle at Leander's chest.

Leander eased back a step. "I'm a patient here," he said, raising his lone arm. "I went down to the river to wash myself."

The guard looked at Leander's uniform and saw the stump at his shoulder. He lowered his weapon, but he still didn't allow him inside. "You know the password?"

Password? He had nearly forgotten they were in Southern territory. He stammered and stuttered as though searching his mind for a lost word, but the word wasn't lost. No one had told him a password.

As the soldier became impatient, Paul reached through the doorway for a water bucket on the porch. "Leander," she said. "Where ya been? Supper's past ready."

"Said he went down to the river to wash," the guard said.

"The river?" Paul's face blanched and her freckles stepped forward. "You was at the river? Jist now?"

27

A NEW DREAM

PAUL VOUCHED FOR LEANDER, AND THE GUARDS LET him inside.

As soon as they were in the room of cots, Paul's voice flared, but her eyes avoided Leander's. "Didn't I tell ya ta stay put? Ya's in Georgia. Best not forget it."

Leander looked down at his feet.

"Not long ago, this here was a Reb hospital," Paul went on. "Plenty of folks in this town ain't happy we's here. They'd as leave shoot ya as look at ya."

"Sorry," Leander mumbled, not sure if his apology was for leaving the hospital or for spying on Paul's nakedness.

Back on his cot, he balanced a tin plate of cold stew on his lap while he spooned it into his mouth. His eyes followed Paul. The girl performed the duties of a hospital steward as though every move were watched by her commander. But why? What made a girl dress like a soldier?

Leander and Lila sat beneath a tall sycamore as the river flowed past them. He took her hand and reached to stroke her fingers with his other hand, but his hand was gone.

Leander woke with a start. His dreams had changed. He no longer had two hands when he dreamed. Sleep wasn't an escape from the nightmare anymore.

28
THE LETTER

YOU CAN TELL 'EM WHEN YOU GET HOME. THAT'S WHAT Given had said about Leander telling his folks he'd lost his arm. But that was weeks ago. Even if Giv hadn't written to Ma and Pa or Nate, he would have written to his own folks. And to Lila. What had he told them?

If Leander was truly a man, he needed to let them know what had happened. He told Paul he was ready to write a letter home. "When you have time," he added politely.

"It'll be easier if'n I have something steady under the paper," Paul said. "Since ya's gittin' around now, how's about we go ta the parlor? There's a table there."

Leander followed Paul, who brought a pen, ink bottle, and paper to a front room off the winding-staircase hall. High-ceilinged like the room with the cots, the parlor looked more like someone's home, with bookshelves beside a deep window and portraits on the papered walls. Paul sat at a small table and motioned for Leander to sit in the chair across from her.

She dipped the pen in ink and brushed its tip along the bottle's edge. "What ya want I should write?"

"It should commence with 'Dear Ma and Pa.' Oh, wait. Make it 'Dear Ma and Pa and Nate.' Nate's my brother."

The pen's tip scratched along the paper. Leander watched as Paul's hand dipped ink and slid across the page. He had often seen her hands wring cloths and dip water. How had he not noticed they were tiny hands, a girl's hands?

"I need to tell them about my accident," he said. Might as well put it in writing and be done with it.

"Accident? Wasn't you shot by Rebs?"

"My gun blew up on me." He watched her write the words. "The barrel got plugged up with mud when I fell, and I forgot to check it before I fired. It was my own fault."

Leander waited for a look of disdain on Paul's face as she wrote the words, but her eyes followed her pen-strokes without a hint of scorn. "What ya want I should say about your arm?"

"Tell them I won't be much use to them now, but I'll try. They deserve better than me."

"Likely, they're jist glad ya's alive. Ya dang near died

when they first brung ya here. Most fellers what git all fever-y like you done end up with the gangrene. It's a hard way ta die."

Was she right? Would they welcome him home even if he couldn't work?

Paul looked up from the letter. "Do ya know how to spell *amputated?*"

Leander laughed. "Just tell them I'm a quarter-foot taller from when I left, but I'm an arm short."

Paul choked back a smile. "How kin ya laugh about it?"

Leander wasn't sure why, but it felt right. He had lost his arm. It was time to reconcile himself to that. And now he had confessed his carelessness to his folks. He had to accept his new life, one without Lila or his right arm. At least it *was* a life.

Paul grinned at him. "I'm right glad ya didn't die from it, on account of I cain't spell *gangrene* neither."

This time Leander's laugh came from deep inside him. He hadn't laughed like that in a very long time, and it felt good.

Paul didn't hold back her own laugh. A tinkly laugh. A girl's laugh. A laugh that filled her pretty face with a spirit that had been a rare sight since his time in the army.

He wanted to tuck that spirit in his pocket and hang onto it forever.

"Tell Nate I'm glad he's working for Doc," Leander went on.

Leander watched as Paul's forehead bunched into small wrinkles of concentration. Leander's gaze followed her hand, her eyes, and her freckled face.

"Nate wants to work and earn enough money to marry Lila. She's his girl." Leander didn't know what made those words pour from his lips. Saying them left a sting on his tongue.

"*Lila*," Paul said. "How ya spell that?"

"You don't have to write that part. I reckon they already know he plans to marry Lila." The sting moved from his tongue and headed toward his heart.

Paul looked up. "This Lila is your brother's girl?"

Leander nodded.

"I thought might be she was *your* girl. Ya called her name in your sleep a time or two. Back when the fever gripped ya."

"I don't have a girl," Leander said. "Lila and me were friends, nothing more." He recognized the truth in his words, a truth he'd never admitted before, even to himself.

This sting went deeper and left a wrenched feeling in his gut.

"Ya want ta say you'll be home afore long?" Paul asked.

"No." The word came out more forcefully than he'd intended. "Best not put it in writing until . . . until I'm for-sure certain about when. I need to be stronger for such a long trip." He wasn't *afraid* to go home. He just wasn't ready yet.

When the letter was finished, they walked back to the room with the cots.

"You work hard here," Leander said. "You're smaller than I am." *And a girl*, he thought. "How do you manage to do it all?"

"Pap says a body kin do what a body wants to, if a body wants to hard enough."

It sounded like something Pa would agree with.

29

PAP

*L*EANDER WAITED ON THE RIVERBANK AS SHE STEPPED *from the water. Wet streams drizzled down her skin, and his breathing quickened. He looked into her freckled face and green eyes.*

Leander woke with a start and felt thick, damp air pressing down on him. Sweat filled every crease of his body, and his clothes stuck to him.

He got up from the sticky cot and looked for Paul. Across the room, she peeled a bloody bandage from a soldier's arm. Her hands tenderly unwound it as she comforted the patient in the soothing tone she always used with the men. Her face glistened with sweat, and her moist skin reminded him of his dream. His dreams had always been about Lila until this one. He waited for the feeling of loss to wrench his gut, but it had loosened its grip.

He wanted to go down to the river to catch a breath of air. He wanted to float in the water and think of home— the home from a year ago. Before Ma and Pa had quit speaking to each other. Before Nate had shattered his legs and Leander had joined the army. Maybe even further back to when he and Lila were young'uns together. But he wasn't a young'un anymore.

He walked over to Paul. "How can I help?"

"I don't need no—"

"I got nothing else to do. How can I help?"

"I gotta dress Fenton's shoulder, but Pap's needin' water."

"I'll get the water."

Paul's smile made Leander feel even warmer than he already was. He hurried outside and found two full buckets on the porch. The burn on his left hand had healed long ago, but the heavy bucket dug its handle into the scar and the old pain reared up. What were those words Paul said her father used? *A body can do what a body wants to, if a body wants to hard enough.* He ignored the pain and lugged the buckets inside one at a time.

This was his life now. Twice as many trips to tote

things, twice as long to do everything. Would he be able to milk a cow with only one hand?

He found a dipper in an empty water pail and plunked it into one of the full buckets.

Paul's father's skin was as hot as a rock in the summer sun, and his breaths came in small gulps and puffs. The cloth from his forehead had fallen to the floor. Leander rinsed it and wrung it out as well as one hand could manage, and held it to the man's face the way he had seen Paul do.

The man groaned, and when his lips parted, Leander offered the dipper. He tipped it gently, waiting to see if the man was able to drink. And he was. He drank about half the dipper before he turned his head away.

"He ain't been drinkin' much for me. Thank ya." Leander hadn't heard Paul come up behind him until she spoke.

"Maybe we should move his cot closer to the window," he said. "If there's fresh air out there, he'll breathe easier."

They tugged and scraped the cot across the wood floor, Leander trying to do his fair share of pulling, even with one arm. When the cot was beneath the open window, they helped Paul's father sit up, and the man's breathing eased a mite.

"Will ya sit with him while I do my work?" Paul asked.

Leander pried his damp collar from his sweaty neck. Thoughts of cool river air flew right out that open window. He sat on the edge of the man's cot and watched Paul. He wondered how a father could allow his daughter to join the army.

Watching the man's face, Leander listened to him breathe, hearing each breath: some quiet, some ragged with the struggle for air. Even if he dared to ask the questions pecking in his brain, the man was not up to answering.

30
DEATH'S VISIT

LEANDER WOKE TO ANOTHER HOT MORNING. HE
saw Paul lugging two heavy water pails and jumped up
to help.

"Why don't ya look after Pap fer me?" she said. "He
took water from ya right well yesterday."

Leander carried one of the pails to the cot by the
window. Pap was asleep, and his skin was cool to the touch
No fever. Leander wanted to yell the news to Paul, but it
could wait. He didn't want to jolt Pap awake, so he dipped
a cloth in water and held it to the man's forehead.

Pap didn't stir. Leander tapped the man's arm. Tapped
it again. Ever so gently, he shook the man's shoulder. The
other shoulder. No sign of life. For a fleeting second, the
face Leander saw was Nate's on the bank of the pond last
summer. He held the dipper near the man's mouth and

nose, hoping to see his breath flutter the water just a little. There! Was that a sign of breathing or was it just Leander's trembling hand that caused the water to shudder?

Leander felt the man's forehead again. Cool to the touch. So were his hands. Almost cold, even in this dreadful heat. Leander felt his wrist, his neck, his chest, seeking a pulse, a heartbeat. He found none.

For a moment, Pa slipped into Leander's mind. How would he feel if this were Pa?

He took a deep breath and edged to where Paul was dressing a soldier's wound.

Paul looked up. "Did he take water fer ya? Is he still afire with the fever?"

Leander shook his head. The girl's eyes searched his, probing them with questions he didn't want to answer.

"I'm sorry," he said, his voice barely a whisper.

He saw the tears gather, watched her refuse to let them fall. She turned back to the soldier and offered him her smile and soothing voice. "There now," she told the patient. "That'll hold ya fer a spell. Lie back and I'll fetch ya some water in an eye-blink. You'll feel good as new afore ya know it."

Her eyes stayed wet, but the girl finished tending the

entire room of men, never once looking over at the cot by the window. How did she summon such strength?

Her duties completed, she sat on the edge of Pap's cot. She leaned close to his face, searching for the same signs of life Leander had. Resigned to the truth, she took hold of Pap's hand and stroked his fingers.

"I wish ya coulda knowed him." Her glistening eyes looked up at Leander. "A better man never drew . . . breath." The last word caught in her throat, and Leander saw the quiver of her chin and the quake in her shoulders.

He sat beside her, put his arm around her, and drew her close. For a second, she leaned into him, but pulled back quickly. Her eyes peeped through wet lashes and her cheeks turned pink.

He dropped his arm. He knew she was a girl, and maybe she suspected he knew, but he had to treat her like the soldier she pretended to be. She deserved that.

31

GRAVESIDE

LEANDER AND PAUL STOOD BESIDE A SMALL CROSS Paul had fashioned from two slender branches of a sweet gum tree.

The privates on burial detail had tried to cart Pap's body to the "dead field," to bury him with the others whose lives had ended in this place so far from their Northern homes. Leander hadn't let them. He'd insisted they bury Pap here, on the edge of the cotton field beside the river. With all the work Paul had done for the hospital, that seemed right.

It had been Leander's idea for Paul to pin a tag to her father's shirt with his name and home state. "In case you decide to move him back to West Virginia after the war."

Now Leander stood beside her, the sounds of the Coosa streaming past them, cool breezes keeping vigil.

"Pap'll like this spot," Paul said. "He al'ys said folks is like rivers, ever a-changin' and ever a-changin' others."

Leander thought about all the changes in the past year. Others had changed him. Had he changed others as well? Had he changed them for the good?

"Pap done ever'thin' fer me, all my life," Paul said. "He taught me ta walk and talk, and made plumb sure I didn't walk too far or talk too loud. Taught me ta creep up on a possum, flush out a rabbit, and shine a deer. He give me my first gun and my first skinnin' knife. Don't know what I'll do without 'im."

Tears gathered again in her eyes. Leander resisted the urge to put his arm around her shoulders, though he truly wanted to.

"I'll give you a moment alone," he told her. Forcing himself to leave her side, he walked along the river. He picked up a pebble and plunked it in his pocket. A glance at Paul showed her head bowed in grief.

He kept walking and found a prettier stone, and put it in his pocket, too. He added more and more of them until his pocket sagged so heavy he feared it would tear. Paul was kneeling now beside the grave.

He had come to care for this girl pretending to be a boy,

even though he knew nothing about her. Surely her name wasn't Paul. He wondered what her real name was, and was she making up those stories about hunting possum, rabbits, and deer? Those didn't sound like things a girl would do. But Leander had never met a girl like Paul.

She stood up and motioned him to her side. He took the pebbles from his pocket and sprinkled them around the cross she had made.

"Just think of them as gravestones," he said, looking into her green eyes.

She cocked her head to one side and gave him a probing look.

He felt uncomfortable, almost as if he were looking at her without her clothes—again. He lowered his eyes to the wooden cross and studied the twine that bound the two pieces together, the twine a daughter had twisted with love.

Paul lifted Leander's chin, and he felt his heart race.

"Thank ya fer helpin' me git him buried proper, in a place he kin find peace." She gave him that scrutinizing look again—a look that made him feel he'd been caught with his thoughts pinned to his shirt.

32

GONE

WHEN LEANDER WOKE, HE SEARCHED THE room for Paul. He had decided to tell her—gently—that he knew her secret, and ask her those questions he craved the answers to. He would ask if she'd write to him when he went home.

But he didn't see her.

The sound of footsteps in the hall wasn't Paul's. A hospital steward strode through the doorway, carrying buckets of water. Leander watched how easily he carried the buckets, showing no sign of their weight. Paul's face might have shown strain when she did that, but she was always willing to share her gracious smile with every patient. Nobody could do this job the same way she did.

Leander listened for her footsteps. The wait grew long, and the steward filled dippers for the men on the cots.

That was Paul's job, and Leander had never seen her take a day off from it.

A thought struck him. This wasn't an ordinary day. Paul had just lost her father. Leander was certain she was standing beside that small cross between the cotton field and the Coosa.

He jumped up from his cot, hurried out the door, and broke into a run as he raced along the cotton field's path. He came around the stalks, saw the cross, and heard the rushing sound of the river. But Paul wasn't there.

She had obviously been there recently, because a bouquet of yellow flowers leaned against the cross. He stared at them as if to ask them where she'd gone.

He trudged back to the room with the flowered wallpaper, the room where he'd grown used to the stench of death.

"I saw you light out," the steward said. "Figured you was heading for the privy. Good to know at least one of you can see to his own body needs."

"Where's Paul?" Leander asked. "Paul Settles, the one who's been doing . . . what you're doing."

"The skinny red-headed squirt who was helping out?"

No, the beautiful red-haired girl who worked hard, Leander thought, but he just nodded.

"Heard he moved out early with a unit joining up with Sherman's troops, heading toward Resaca or maybe Atlanta."

"No! That can't be. That . . ." But in his heart, he knew the truth of it. She'd said weeks ago she had stayed to take care of Pap, that caring for him was what kept her from going back to the fighting. She had been a devoted daughter. And now, true to her word, she had gone back. That was Paul. Doing her duty.

The thought that he'd never see her again stabbed through his heart. He'd never be able to ask why she'd joined the army, or even who she really was.

He dreamed of her at night. He was certain she'd be in his dreams for a long time, but dreaming wasn't enough. He wanted to get to know the real girl behind the green eyes; wanted to spend time with the girl who showed kindness to the soldiers she tended, the girl who scolded or teased him one minute and showed her soft, sweet side the next. He wanted to hold her and tell *her* sweet things. And now he'd never be able to.

He remembered the things she had told him, things about changing folks. He had tried not to think about how *his* actions had changed Ma and Pa. He had thought about proving he was a man. He'd avoided going home to face them, even though he'd been well enough to travel for more than a week.

But he'd proved nothing. A man didn't leave his pa to tend a farm alone. A man didn't cause his ma more pain than she'd already suffered. A man would go home and make things right with his folks.

I need to be a man, he thought. *I can't let that girl-pretending-to-be-a-boy be more of a man than I am.*

PART TWO

POLLY

33

LEAVING

POLLY SETTLES GRABBED HER BEDROLL, HAVERSACK, AND knife, along with Pap's smoothbore flintlock musket. She patted the pocket where she kept Ma's ring. It was the only thing of Ma's she possessed—except for her red hair and freckles.

She peeked around the doorway into the back room of the hospital, where she'd tended patients for more than two months. In the dim light, she saw Leander asleep on his cot. She hated to leave without telling him she was going, but partings caused misery. And Leander was the reason she had to leave.

As she watched him sleep, she felt her lips turn up at the sight of him. She could no longer deny she had feelings for him. But Pap had always said feelings were for girls.

If she were to pass for a boy, she'd need to hide those feminine notions.

She'd come close to spilling her secret to Leander when they'd stood by Pap's grave, when she'd told him Pap had taught her to hunt. She'd almost said Pap had also taught her to piece a shirt, mend a cuff, sew on a patch, and make over the dresses in Ma's trunk to fit her.

Perhaps Leander had already guessed she was a girl. When he'd pulled her close after Pap passed, there seemed to be something more than simple comforting in his one-armed embrace.

It scared her. The army had no place for a girl. And an orphaned girl had no place in the world. She had to remain a boy.

Did Leander truly suspect? Better not to know. Better to leave without more words. Better not to be close to him and tempted to confess. Better not to have those *feelings*.

She broke off a handful of yellow tansies from beside the privy path and toted them to Pap's grave. In the waning moonlight, she took off her cap and set the flowers against the cross.

Her fingers brushed against the pebbles Leander had collected and scattered around the cross. She picked up one of them and rolled it in her hand. It was rough on one side and smooth on the other. She stood up and plunked it into her pocket, heard it clink against Ma's ring. Leander had gathered the stones for Pap. She could take this one reminder of the two she was leaving behind.

"It weren't s'posed to end like this," she said to the night air. The air brushed her cheek and ruffled through her hair. She choked back her tears. Tears were for girls.

"I cain't stay here, Pap. And I cain't go home. I gotta keep bein' Paul and go where nobody'll pay me mind, where I'm jist one more flea on a dog. Cain't vow I'll be back, but I reckon you'll keep your eye on me. You al'ys did. And, Pap, keep your eye on Leander, too."

34

DON'T THINK ABOUT PAP

*D*ON'T THINK ABOUT *P*AP, POLLY TOLD HERSELF. Leander wasn't the only reason she had to leave the place where a cross and a grave were constantly threatening to cause those feminine tears.

She hurried to catch up with a passel of Indiana infantry fixing to march out of Rome, Georgia. Their sergeant had accepted the seasoned West Virginia boy-soldier, but brooked no shirkers. He was in an all-fired hurry to get to wherever they were going.

Polly's feet marched beside other soldiers' feet—bigger feet at the ends of longer legs. Keeping pace with the rhythm of the drum corps, they quickly covered hard dirt roads beneath chestnuts, elms, and hickories. Hurrying left no time to feel the shade. No time to take more than scant notice of hardscrabble farms, where threadbare, bleak-faced families stared as they marched by.

She tried not to think about Pap, and the sound of marching made it impossible to hear the tiny *clink* from the pebble and the ring. But putting one foot in front of the other, over and over, left her mind open for thinking. And remembering. Pap had been her whole life since the day Polly was born.

When Virginia seceded and war commenced, Pap held firm with keeping the Union whole. He'd talked of joining the army, but he couldn't leave Polly, with no ma to look after her. The war was already in its third year when West Virginia became a state, separate from Virginia and loyal to the Union. If West Virginia had the courage to stand up against the Rebellion, Pap wanted to do more than mend harnesses and cut hay. He yearned to join the fight.

He struck a deal with Miz Fletcher, the same Miz Fletcher who'd always told him she could make Polly into a *real lady*. Pap offered her their yearling colt if Polly could live with her until he came back.

But no one asked Polly how she felt. If a *real lady* was what Miz Fletcher was, Polly wanted no part of it. So when Pap left to join the army, Polly cut off her long red hair, pulled on a pair of his trousers, slipped away from Miz Fletcher, and followed him. Pap tried to send her home, warned her it wasn't safe for a girl in the army. Not only was it illegal, but soldiers at war sometimes did unspeakable things to girls.

Polly dug in both heels. Pap argued and she argued back.

"I won't stay with Miz Fletcher," she said, standing her ground with both hands on her trousered hips. "Druther curl up in a hole with wild critters than live in her ladied-up house."

Finally Pap relented. "I reckon I raised ya too much like a son ta change ya now," he said.

They stopped on the banks of the Kanawha, and Pap dunked her as if he were a preacher and christened her *Paul*. They'd go to war together—father and son. The army was desperate for soldiers, and recruiters didn't look too close at the "son."

It wasn't easy, but Pap made it possible. They shared a tent, and when she had her monthly lady's time, Pap saw to it she got a bit of privacy. He kept an eye out so she could take a quick bath in a stream every few weeks or so without the men catching wise. He treated her like a boy and kept others believing she was.

Without Pap, could she convince folks she was Paul? Without a father, would she still look like a son? She had to. She couldn't go back to being Polly. Polly Settles was as good as dead, and maybe *dead* was best.

If a Rebel ball pierced her heart, would they bury her without looking close at what lay beneath her uniform?

35

FORAGING

OLLY'S NEW UNIT MARCHED DEEPER INTO GEORGIA. The fighting was closer now, and she often heard cannon fire in the distance. And they headed toward it.

The sergeant pushed the troops harder. If they covered ten miles one day, he demanded twelve the next. But marching was good. As long as they were on the move, it was easier to avoid conversation with the men who marched shoulder-to-shoulder with her. Polly's shoulder was nearer to their elbows, but she wore her bravest soldier face and marched. Her legs ached from marching, but that was good, too. It distracted her from the empty place in her heart.

She shared a tent with a man named Fox, a man who toted a Bible and prayed every night. He kept to himself and did most of his talking to the Lord. That sat just fine with Polly.

When supply wagons failed to get through, hardtack became every meal's staple. There was still coffee to dip it into, but the coffee seemed to get a mite watery as the march grew endless. The empty place in Polly's heart had a matching one in her belly.

As hot June days melted into hotter July ones, Polly felt she might disappear like the steam that rose from the coffeepot every morning. She almost wished she could.

At the end of a long day's march, Fox asked if Polly wanted to join a foraging party. "Me, Crawford, and Morgan," he said. "And you, if you want."

She had noticed Crawford, who sat by the fire every night playing a mouth organ. Morgan was a tad older than most of the men, and carried a tintype photograph of his daughter. She had seen him show it to the others. They seemed like nice men, so she agreed. She tucked her knife in the waistband of her trousers, in case they came across some game.

Dusk was still hours away, so they stayed off the main road, stepping over roots of oaks and maples, until Polly spotted a peach orchard. Not one peach remained on the trees. A cornfield was also picked clean.

Polly caught sight of a barn just beyond the trees, and pointed. "Look there."

"Could be the corn and peaches are inside," Fox said.

"Any farmer what picked his crop green don't want nobody to find it," Polly said. "We best be keerful." She knew it would be stealing, but the thought of a juicy peach—even a green one—put that thought right out of her mind.

They strapped their canteens tightly against their bodies, so as not to make a sound, and crept up to the barn. Polly pressed her ear against the rough siding. All was quiet.

They stayed close to the building as they came around it. A house sat at the opposite end of the farmyard, but Polly saw no lamplight in the windows, no dog on the porch, no sign of life.

"You're smallest, Settles," Morgan told Polly. "Less likely to be spotted. We'll wait here."

Polly crouched low and hurried to the barn's open door. She knew about farmers. If the door had been left open, the farm was abandoned or the farmer was nearby. If abandoned, it was unlikely they'd find food inside. And she didn't want to come face-to-face with the farmer. In his eyes, she'd be nothing more than a Yankee thief, worthy of being shot.

But the others depended on her—and something substantial to eat was mighty tempting. She slipped inside the barn.

The waning daylight stayed close to the door, and Polly stepped slowly into the shadows. As her eyes adjusted to the dimness, she looked into stalls with empty feed bins. No livestock. Bushel baskets lay upended. Empty. She even climbed a ladder to the loft, but found nothing more than a few scattered remnants of hay. She wasn't hungry enough to eat hay   yet.

She heard a rustle, a sound so tiny she reckoned it was a mouse. Not exactly the game she had hoped for, but any critter might be worth finding. She held her breath and listened, but heard only the rapid thumping of her heart.

Turning to climb back down the ladder, she listened again. This time, she heard the familiar sound of a rifle being cocked. The farmer!

36
CAPTURED

"GET DOWN OFF THAT LADDER AND DON'T move," a man's voice ordered.

"How can I git off'n the ladder if'n I don't move?" she said, hoping the farmer was good-natured.

When her feet reached the barn floor, she turned to face him. But the man with a bushy mustache was no farmer. Even in the dim light, she recognized his Reb uniform. His rifle was pointed straight at her, and his finger was on the trigger. Her breath caught in her throat. Was this how she would die? Where were Fox, Crawford, and Morgan?

But the Reb didn't pull the trigger. He marched her outside, where Fox, Crawford, and Morgan were lined up against the barn, facing other Confederate rifles.

"Why, yours ain't nothing but a sprout," one of the Rebs said. "Keep a good eye on him." The man laughed.

"If he was a fish, I'd throw him back," the first Reb said.

"A fish? He ain't big enough fer bait."

One Reb confiscated her musket and canteen, while another tied Polly's hands behind her back. Fox, Crawford, and Morgan were already tied, and the Rebs looped and knotted a rope around each of their ankles, leaving less than a yard of rope between them. There was no hope of escape without all four of them doing it together.

Her survival as a boy had depended on staying separate and private. Polly would have just as soon been shot.

What would Pap do if he were here? Pap hated Rebs. But Pap wouldn't have been captured. He was shrewd. Was he looking down at her, shaking his head in disappointment?

"They sneaked up on us from behind," Crawford whispered. "No warning a'tall."

Never lowering his rifle, the man with the bushy mustache marched the prisoners toward the house. No dogs barked. No chickens clucked in the grass. Polly was certain no farmer would come home from his fields to find them. No one knew where they were except these Rebs.

The door of the house stood ajar and creaked on its hinges as a Reb nudged it open with the butt of his rifle. Inside, he lit a lantern and hung it on a peg. The flame's flicker cast lights and shadows across the Rebs' faces, making them appear ghostly. Polly would rather have encountered a ghost.

A table by the window held a bottle of whiskey and two haversacks. A few bedrolls lined the floor. A portrait of a lady hung askew over the mantel. Her eyes seemed to scold Polly for letting herself be captured.

Polly stood between Fox and Morgan, feeling their fear without even touching them. Was her own fear so plain-faced?

The prisoners were ordered to sit in the far corner of the room. With her hands tied, Polly had to slide down the wall to the rough plank floor. She was glad she'd relieved herself before the foraging party headed out. She'd have no way to do that now.

Would the sergeant miss the four of them before morning muster? Would he list them as deserters? Were searchers looking for them? How many other Rebs were nearby? Would Polly's life end in this place?

The captors sat at the table and pulled hardtack from a haversack. They dipped it into cups of whiskey to soften it. Forgetting how tired she was of hardtack, Polly yearned for a bite.

The Rebs filled their cups again. Polly saw the whiskey's effect take hold. Laughter bounced off the walls, and the

Rebs shouted insults at the prisoners—and at the lady's portrait on the wall. Polly's size was cause for jokes. Better they laugh at her for being a small boy than realize she wasn't one at all.

Make me strong, Pap, she said to his image inside her head. *If I die here, let me die brave.*

Pap didn't answer, but she felt stronger, able to think more clearly. Maybe the Rebs would get drunk enough to pass out, and the prisoners could escape. She could cut the ropes with the knife in her waistband—if her tied hands could reach it.

She needed to be shrewd like Pap.

37

FORCED MARCH

THE WHISKEY BOTTLE WAS EMPTY. A REB RAISED his arm to throw it at the prisoners, and Polly flinched. Laughing, the man hurled it at the portrait. The portrait-lady's stern expression showed no fear as the bottle shattered and rained broken glass onto the mantel. Polly needed to be fearless. Or at least look the part.

One by one, the Rebs plopped down on bedrolls and began to snore. Except the one with the bushy mustache. He stood by the door, rifle in hand. His eyes scanned the group of prisoners and stopped on Polly.

She remembered Pap's warning. Soldiers at war sometimes did unspeakable things to girls. Did she look like a girl? Would he do the unspeakable? She drooped her chin and hunched her shoulders to flatten her chest a mite. With her hands tied behind her back, it made her shoulders ache. Better to endure the pain than to suffer the consequences of being discovered.

★ ★ ★

She didn't know she'd fallen asleep until she was awakened by a rifle barrel against her cheek.

"Get up, Runt. We's movin' out."

It wasn't easy to get off the floor. Polly shinnied up the wall with her forearms and elbows, but after sleeping with her legs under her, they buckled. As Fox, tied beside her, struggled to stand, she lost her balance.

The mustached Reb grabbed her arm, yanking her to her feet. The rope at her wrists dug into her flesh as he tightened his grip. His eyes raked across her face and fear prickled her skin.

I'm a boy, I'm a boy, I'm a boy. She said the words over and over in her head, as if to make them true.

As the man's hand lingered on her arm, Polly squinted up at him, trying to summon her deepest, gruffest voice. "You ain't the kind ta hanker after boys, is ya?"

One of the Rebs laughed and the man reached back his hand to strike her, but he stopped and let go of her arm. "You sure is a young one, ain't ya? Your mama know you're playin' soldier?"

Polly bit back the retort that jumped to her tongue.

153

"Ma's dead," she said instead.

Rifles pointed at them, the prisoners were marched outside, still connected by the rope. They walked toward a dusty road that stretched into the distance. The pink sky of dawn to their left showed they were headed south, farther from Union troops.

Polly tried to think shrewd thoughts, but her thoughts told her escape wasn't possible. Not now. Her feet scraped along the red dirt, her legs weak. She couldn't slow down. The prisoners were lashed so close together she had to stay in step with Fox in front of her or be trampled by Morgan from behind.

The heat rose as the sun did. Sweat burned Polly's eyes. She felt it trickle down her neck and back, while her mouth felt as dry as the dust her feet kicked up.

The Rebs took swigs from their canteens as they walked and stopped twice to offer water to the prisoners. Polly drank enough to ease her thirst, but no more. Too much water and she'd need to relieve herself. She'd have no way to do that in private while she was tied between Fox and Morgan.

With the sun directly overhead, the Rebs stopped in the shade of an elm. They fed pieces of hardtack to the prisoners and gave them each a drink.

The Reb with the mustache held the canteen to Polly's lips and tipped it slowly, almost gently. "This war's goin' eat you up. Shoulda stayed at home."

"Ain't got no home."

He shook his head. "God have mercy on ya. You'll need it."

Two Rebs stood guard over them, while the other two scouted ahead. Maybe four prisoners could overtake two Rebs. Polly tried to reach her knife, but couldn't quite do it. The rope around her wrists bit into her skin as she struggled against it.

She looked at the other prisoners. Maybe one of them could get free. Fox lowered his eyes, and Polly reckoned he was talking to the Lord. Morgan watched the road, but Crawford twitched and changed position. Maybe he was having better luck with his bonds.

"You going to let me answer nature's call?" he said.

He wasn't the only one. Polly could no longer ignore the feeling inside her. She needed to go, too.

The Rebs untied the prisoners one at a time and allowed them to relieve themselves under the elm, a rifle barrel at their backs the whole time.

When they untied Polly, she wondered if she could grab her knife and stab the Reb before he fired. Not likely.

And the other rifle was pointed at her, too. She didn't stand a chance against both of them. If she ran, she'd be shot, but maybe death was better than what they would do if they found out she was a girl.

"I need to do more'n make water," she said, and the Rebs let her squat beside the elm. Legs quivering, and thankful for the concealing length of her uniform jacket, she slipped her knife from her waistband, careful to keep it hidden.

Where could she hide it? Beneath the cover of her jacket, she lowered her trousers and opened her drawers. As she emptied her innards, she slid the knife, sheath and all, into her boot.

38

THE TRAIN

HE AFTERNOON'S MARCH ENDED AT RAILROAD tracks, where a locomotive took on water from a spout. Polly saw a long line of freight cars hitched behind it—and the cars were alive! Voices came from deep within them, low murmured voices and moans.

The mustached Reb untied Polly's hands and handed her canteen to her. "God have mercy on ya," he told her again.

As she was loaded into a freight car, her mind lingered on his words. She was in enemy hands. Would God's mercy be enough?

The source of the car's voices sat before her. Union men. A horde of them. The smell of sweat and waste filled the car, and brought the hospital in Rome to mind. That place had gotten Polly used to the disgusting smells that human beings created, but memories of the hospital brought thoughts of Pap—and of Leander. How she wished she had stayed there.

Morgan made his way through the swarm of men, who reached toward him, clutched at him, and pelted him with questions.

The sight of all those hands reaching and touching made Polly stay near the door. She sank onto a thin scattering of damp hay, and its urine smell told her why it was damp.

The Rebs slid the car door closed with a rumble, a scrape, and a bang, and the prisoners were left crammed together like tinned beans. And it was near as dark as being inside a can.

She couldn't see the others, but voices flung questions.

"Where are we?"

"What unit you with?"

"Indiana Infantry," Fox said, "but Settles here is West Virginia."

"We're Army of the Potomac," a voice said. "We been riding in these cars for three days."

"Four," another voice corrected.

"This is Georgia," Morgan said. "Last I heard, we . . ."

The rest of Morgan's words were lost as a whistle

shrieked and the train wheels moved beneath them. They gathered speed with a roaring sound, and the car swayed and rattled Polly's teeth. Hearing voices over the noise of the train was impossible, but Polly knew the body leaning against hers was Fox, and she sensed he was praying.

The stuffy railroad car was hot, filled with moist breath from the men. The foul smells grew stronger as the car cooked in the Georgia sun. Polly would have shed her wool jacket, but she wanted more than her broadcloth blouse between her and these men.

Tiny prickles of light seeped through cracks, and Polly's eyes grew accustomed to the darkness. She saw shapes and shadows of the breathers around her. She pushed her nose close to one of the cracks in search of outside air. Men around her stretched out their limbs as best they could, paying no mind to whether they spread out across two or three others. Polly curled up, protecting her feminine parts.

The dark car grew darker, and daytime's unbearable heat eased only a tad. But the car's stench filled Polly's nostrils no matter what the hour.

Pap had always told her that the way through dark times was with pleasant thoughts. She thought back to Leander at the hospital. She definitely should have stayed there. None of this would have happened. And what lay ahead? What would the Rebs do? Fear overpowered pleasant thoughts.

When she dozed, dreams of Leander filled her head. She stood with him beside the Coosa, listening to the river's sounds.

The feeling that woke her was a familiar one of pressure inside her. She tried to take her mind off it. She thought about how she'd babbled on and on to Leander at Pap's grave. Words had spilled out of her, even though Pap had warned her that keeping her secret would be easier if she stayed quiet. But she'd felt safe talking to Leander. He was close to her age, but it was more than that. She had liked him right off.

She recalled how he'd claimed the girl whose name he'd called out in his feverish sleep was his brother's girl. She hadn't believed it. She suspected he was green jealous of that brother—what was his name again?

She recollected holding her finger to his lips to quiet his cries, lest he wake the other patients. Not only had he stopped calling the girl's name, but he'd kissed Polly's fingertip. She reckoned he'd thought it was that other girl's finger, but she'd liked the feel of it all the same. No one but Pap had ever kissed her. Leander made her wonder what a real kiss felt like. Not just Pap's fatherly kiss or a feverish fingertip kiss. But the kind between a man and a woman. Would she die never knowing that feeling?

Nothing took her mind off the need to go. She tried again, thinking of Fowlers Gap. She recalled hunting and fishing with Pap. She remembered his voice in her head, but that voice was getting harder to recollect.

She couldn't bear it any longer. She had to go! The dark would keep her secret. She dropped her trousers, opened her drawers, and added to the car's smells.

39

DARKER STILL

INTO THEIR SECOND DAY ON THE TRAIN, THE CAR STOPPED. Rebs yanked them from its dark cavity into blinding sunlight, and Polly squinted and struggled to see.

As her eyes adjusted to daylight, she got her first real glimpse of the men from the cars. Some didn't look much older than she was. Some wore bloody bandages and could barely stand. All wore the same expression of a critter caught in a trap.

Pap's voice sounded in her head. *A body kin do what a body wants to—if a body wants to hard enough.*

I want ta be strong, Pap, but I don't think I kin. I'm tryin' not ta be scared, but . . .

Reb soldiers unloaded the cars. Hundreds of Union men spilled onto the wooden railroad platform, filling it and the ground around it. On the other side of the tracks, buildings clustered together to form a town.

Above the town, clouds gathered. They shielded Polly's eyes from the sun, as Reb soldiers marched the Union prisoners away from the town and down a spongy dirt road. In the distance, tall pines reached into the sky. Polly thought of their fragrant scent and hoped the breeze would carry it her way. But all she smelled was the sea of filthy men. And she reckoned she smelled no better.

At a fork in the road, they were halted before a small wooden building. A bearded Reb captain, pale-faced, stoop-shouldered, and wearing shiny boots, stood on the porch and watched as other Rebs counted the troops. One wrote their names in a ledger.

"Paul Settles, Indiana Infantry," she said. She'd been with them nearly a month now. She didn't know the whereabouts of any of her original West Virginia unit, except for the ones buried in Rome—one beneath a cross on the bank of the Coosa.

The prisoners were designated by number to a detachment, a squad, and a mess. The numbers told Polly there were about seven hundred of them. They were to be confined in a prison called Camp Sumter, and the town was Andersonville.

Prison. With hundreds of other prisoners. Male prisoners.

Male guards. *Make me strong, Pap.* But she feared all the strength in the world wouldn't be enough.

The tall pines watched as the seven hundred were marched down a road. They passed a building that smelled of baking bread. The delicious scent seeped through the unwashed hundreds, and hunger gnawed at Polly's innards.

Until they passed another building.

Ragged blankets hung from poles to form a three-sided lean-to of sorts. A roof trimmed with pine brush sheltered piles of. . . . A new stench pelted Polly. The piles were corpses. Her stomach would have emptied—if there'd been anything in it. She struggled to keep back the bile that pushed into her throat.

"Dead house," mumbled one of the prisoners.

They reached the gates of a huge stockade of upright yellow pine trunks, set in the ground side by side, like a silent army. Reb soldiers stood at guard posts along the tops of those pine sentries. Soldiers with guns. Guns that could have picked them off like fish in a puddle. Not far from the dead house.

Polly stayed beside Fox as they were squeezed between men much taller than she was to pass through a gate. And another gate, an inner gate. She couldn't see her new surroundings over the men's heads. Gasps and murmurs swirled around her and multiplied. She heard fear in the voices, but couldn't see what frightened them.

Once well inside the stockade, the mass of men spread out a mite, and Polly saw the reason for the gasps. Not far from the gate, a crossbeam stretched across lumber support posts, and a man was tying nooses to the beam.

40

THE STOCKADE

OX, CRAWFORD, AND MORGAN WERE IN POLLY'S
assigned mess, and she stayed close. They stared at the
gallows. Fox pulled his Bible from his haversack and
prayed. Morgan put his hand on the pocket where he kept
his daughter's photograph.

"Don't know who they's fixin' ta hang," Polly said, "but
it ain't us. Or why'd they assign us to a mess?" But the
others couldn't turn their eyes from that structure of death.

Polly slipped from between them, edging away from
the smell of men for a breath of clean air. But outside that
crowd of men she'd come in with were a heap more men—
and no clean air.

The stockade was good-sized, close to twenty acres by
Polly's guess, but its high walls managed to hold in every

foul odor she could imagine. The filthy stench of human waste, disease, and rotting flesh pressed against her, while outside the walls, those tall trees hoarded their piney scent.

Tents and makeshift shelters cluttered nearly every inch of the camp, even two low hillsides that straddled a scummed-over stream. Thousands of shelters, some mere blankets on poles.

Polly hoped the nasty stream wasn't their drinking water. In the midst of a swamp, it was putrid green and reeked of human waste. A narrow channel at one end formed board "sinks," an open place for prisoners to answer nature's call. Alive with flies, the stream flowed through to catch the droppings.

Smells told Polly that men relieved themselves in other parts of the camp, too. The stockade was like a twenty-acre privy. And those sinks would offer no privacy, so Polly reckoned she'd be one who used other parts of the giant privy.

She'd be hard pressed to find privacy *anywhere* in this prison. The seven hundred she'd arrived with were swallowed up by the massive crowd, tens of thousands who gaped at the gallows. They wore ragged remnants of Union uniforms on bodies with no more meat than a dog's bone. Polly remembered the building that smelled of bread. Few men inside the stockade looked as if they'd had much bread—or anything else to eat.

As she watched the haggard faces, a drop of water hit the tip of her nose. After two more drops plopped onto her hand, the clouds emptied. It was the kind of hard rain Pap called a gully-washer, and every gully, ditch, and hole in this godforsaken place needed washing.

Polly didn't look for shelter, but took off her hat and let the rain run down her neck and soak through her uniform and drawers. Her skin welcomed the feel of it. She uncorked her canteen and held it in her outstretched hands, knowing every drop that found its way inside would be one more drop of clean drinking water. She even threw back her head and let rainwater run right down her throat, easing her parched tongue enough to keep it from sticking to the roof of her mouth.

When the rain backed off, Polly capped her canteen. Red mud sucked at her boots as she rejoined Fox and the others. Their clothes hung on them like wet mops, and Morgan's hair dripped into his eyes. Polly reckoned she looked likewise.

"We need to build a shelter," Morgan said. "One of

the Army of the Potomac fellers says he'll sell us a rubber blanket."

"Sell?" Fox said. "We got to *buy* a dang blanket?"

"We need shelter, a place to keep dry in the next rain."

"And shade," Crawford added. "This Georgia sun is heaps hotter than Indiana."

Even though she'd been wearing her hat most of the time, Polly's fair skin had toughened during her time in the army, but she knew that it would burn to blisters in constant sun. She pulled a few coins from her pocket to add to those Morgan held.

As Morgan counted the money in his hand, somber music came from outside the stockade and put a chill in the air. The "Dead March"! Polly looked up to the six nooses tied to the crossbeam.

41

THE HANGING

THE STOCKADE GATES OPENED AND A SMALL BAND marched in, a Union band. Behind them, Reb guards escorted six prisoners in Union uniforms. What crimes had led to this? Being killed in battle was part of war, but being hanged was heartless.

The shiny-booted captain rode a white mare behind the six. A priest walked beside him. The captain's pale face showed no sign of feeling as he turned the prisoners over to another man, gave his mare a slight kick, and disappeared with his guards beyond the gate.

"Just like Pilate," Fox said, patting his Bible.

The condemned men's hands were bound, and they climbed to the gallows. One bolted and slashed his way through the throng with a dagger. He made it as far as the putrid stream before he was recaptured and dragged back to the others. How had he hoped to escape the solid stockade walls?

Polly thought about the knife in her boot. Having a knife hadn't saved that man. Escape seemed unlikely. But she'd bide her time and watch and wait.

The men on the scaffold were each given a chance to speak, but from where she stood, Polly couldn't hear their words.

She had heard last words from dozens of men at the hospital. Likely these were similar. Most had asked Polly to write to loved ones, some had cursed the Rebs or the war, and one had poured out his mistakes as if she were a priest hearing his sins.

She didn't know what Pap's last words had been, couldn't even remember the last time he'd spoken her name. She'd always reckoned he'd open his eyes one day and be well again. But it hadn't happened. Nobody left to look after Polly except Polly. And she wasn't going to let herself end up like those six.

Now, she listened to mumbled voices around her and looked up at the gallows. The priest prayed over the condemned and a drummer's beat seemed to grip Polly's heart in its rhythm. Nooses were placed around the six necks. Just as a man was about to kick out props from beneath the planks that held the men, Polly turned her head. She had no hankering to see more death than she had already witnessed in her nearly sixteen years.

The drumming stopped. She heard a thump, and the sound of wood on wood. A collective breath from the masses told her the deed was done. Silence dropped over the camp like a net over prey. Inside the solid wall of upright pines, she felt like prey. How could she hope to get out of this place? Cannons stood atop a hill outside one corner of the stockade, looking quiet but capable.

The silence disappeared into a cloud of noise, akin to the sound of an army camp, but different. Strange languages and unfamiliar accents joined the usual voices. And the tone of the voices held no trace of hope.

A distance from the creek, where the sloping bank leveled off, Polly spotted a campfire's smoke and a dark-faced man sitting beside the fire, his arms around his knees. So she wasn't the only one who'd had no desire to watch the hanging. The man sat in front of a shelter that looked stronger than most, with blanket walls and a roof of pine boughs. He beckoned her over with his hand.

When she reached him, she realized he was younger than he'd looked from afar, probably not yet twenty, as much a boy as a man. He took off his hat and fanned the fire as he nodded a greeting. His face was dark only where the fire's black smoke had stained it. His hair was blond, his ears and forehead as white as hers.

"What'd they do?" she asked. "The ones who was hanged? Do the Rebs hang considerable many?"

"Rebs didn't hang them," the man said. "We did."

42

THE MAN BY THE FIRE

POLLY'S MOUTH DROPPED OPEN. "YOU?"

"The prisoners here. Tried, convicted, and sentenced them. They were raiders. Stole food, clothes, firewood, cook-pots, whatever they could find. Started fights, gave beatings, didn't care who they hurt. Wasn't safe to close your eyes, lest you wake up to find yourself stripped naked and empty-handed."

Polly gasped.

"We got us a police force now," the man said. "Hopin' they'll keep things a tad more civil."

Polly looked around. "Civil? Here?"

"A tad. But days'll come when you might think being hanged is better than living in this wretched place. I seen more than one man cross the dead-line to end his suffering."

"Dead-line?"

"That rail inside the walls." He pointed to a fence that resembled a high hitching rail, about a dozen feet inside the stockade walls. "You go beyond that, and one of them guards up in a pigeon roost will shoot you before you take another step."

She blew out her breath. "This place don't seem no better'n hell itself."

"Worse than hell." The man grinned. "I hear Old Satan escaped weeks ago."

Polly tried to smile at his joke, but her lips wouldn't do it. "Do many escape?"

"They try. Always a tunnel bein' dug somewhere, but the Rebs send out dogs, drag 'em back, and put 'em in the stocks. Or the dead house."

As Polly remembered that morbid building outside the gate, bile lurched toward her throat again. The knife in her boot felt heavy and useless.

The man fanned his fire. "Some get paroled. Like the burial detail. Dying's easy. Ain't so easy to get 'em all buried. The ones that get paroled have to swear an oath to the Confederacy."

"Don't reckon I could turn Reb. Even to be freed," Polly

said. She knew Pap never would have.

"I seen ya catching rainwater. That's smart. Water from that stream likely killed a good many. It's best upstream, where it comes into the prison, but close to the dead-line. Me? I boil my water." The man nodded toward a kettle on his fire. "Then it don't smell or taste so bad. If you feel sick, keep it quiet. Their hospital is the last stop before the dead house."

The man's eyes raked over Polly, his look sympathetic. Why was he telling her this? Did every new arrival get the same advice?

"Firewood ration's been pretty scant," he went on. "Save it for cooking and boiling water. You won't need it for heat until the weather turns cold."

Cold weather? It was July. How long would she be here?

"Now and again, I get my hands on firewood from digging," he said. "If you run short, I might can spare a little."

"You *dig* for firewood?"

"Must've been pines here before they built the prison. All gone now except them two-three pines up yonder." The man nodded toward a couple scraggly pines in one corner of the camp. "I dig with a tin cup for old roots.

Firewood's precious. When they haul down those raiders' bodies, men'll swarm all over the lumber from the gallows, sellin' it to willing buyers."

"Ain't got much money," Polly said. "Just put in with my messmates ta buy a rubber blanket fer shelter, fer four of us."

"If it gets too crowded under your blanket, you can stay here. I got room. Nobody else cares to share my little shebang."

Polly squinted and looked from the man's face to his shelter. "Why's that?"

"Smallpox."

She backed away three hurried steps.

"Not me," the man said. "Fellers who lived here before me, but they all been dead a while. Knowing the pox was here scares off most. But I been here for weeks, and . . ." He pushed up his shirt sleeves and held out his arms. "No pox."

"I best git back ta my mess." Polly turned to walk away.

"Hey!" the man called. "What name you go by?"

"Paul Settles."

"A man's name. That's good." He winked at her. "I'll keep your secret."

Polly's heart nearly leapt from her chest. "Got no secret."

Her voice sounded shrill, even to her own ears. "No secret," she said again in a lower, deeper voice.

He looked around them and said in a whisper, "I lived with my ma and sister long enough to recognize a *she* when I see one. But I won't tell."

She tried to hide the hard thumping beneath her breasts. "Nothin' ta tell."

43
SECRETS AND SHLETER

DON'T WORRY," THE MAN SAID. "YOUR SECRET'S safe with me."

"What give ya the notion . . . fool notion . . . that I . . . ? But I ain't."

"When you throwed back your head to catch rainwater on your tongue, I suspicioned it. When your uniform soaked through, I knew certain. You're dry now, and it ain't so easy to tell. Slump your shoulders. Stay dry. And try to grow a beard." He laughed.

Polly didn't even smile.

She watched him ladle water from his kettle into a wooden pail. "When your canteen gets empty, come by and refill it. Some wells ain't much better than the stream. And come back here if anyone threatens you. You'll be safe with me."

Polly didn't feel safe. She slumped her shoulders and headed back toward Fox, looking over her shoulder more than once. She remembered Pap's warning, and thought about the knife in her boot. She had never used it on anything bigger than a rabbit.

★ ★ ★

The new prisoners pitched rows of tents and shelters in the red mud, soon swallowed up by the endless sea of tents. Polly watched Morgan and Crawford attach the blanket to two poles, lean-to fashion. Other shelters loomed close— smotheringly close.

"Bought this wood from a sutler up near the other gate," Morgan said. "Left over from the gallows, but it works for tent poles. Money won't last long if we got to buy all we need. The sutler says he'll take most any kind of goods in payment, so we ought to pony up what we have before we decide what to buy."

Polly thought about Ma's ring in her pocket, and noticed Crawford didn't mention his mouth organ. "All I got is a few coins," she lied. Her knife was fixing to stay secret. Pap had given it to her, and it was her only chance to protect herself.

"Our little shelter's going to be tight as bark on a tree," Crawford said, "but it's better than no shelter a'tall."

"Looks like we'll need to take turns keeping out of the rain," Fox said.

Polly remembered what the man by the fire had said about staying dry. *You can stay here. I got room.* Did his offer to share his sleeping place have something to do with her being a girl? That thought scared her even more than smallpox. But she couldn't risk getting soaked to the skin again, either.

She needed to escape, but if escape were possible, why had so many not been able to do it?

The sun disappeared behind the tall pines outside the gate, and the stockade grew dark. Thousands of daytime voices ebbed to a nighttime hum. Crawford's mouth organ sang in the moonlight, and another mouth organ answered. The black sky stretched above and hid the horrid sights, but the smells couldn't be masked.

Polly cursed herself for getting captured. She was hungry. She longed for Pap and Leander. She'd need to keep an eye on the blond man who had scared her witless.

Curled up half-in, half-out of the small shelter, she scratched an itch and reached into her boot. She slid her knife from its sheath and gripped its handle. Ready.

Fear and itches tormented her. The tiniest sounds made

her jump. Did the blond man know where her shelter was? Had he told her secret to others? How could she sleep in this place?

A guard atop the wall called out, "Ten o'clock and all's well!" The next guard repeated the call, and the next, and the next. *All's well? No chance of that.*

When they called the midnight hour, Polly still lay awake. Slogging past mud holes, she eased down the slope to the stream. She had to use the sinks after dark, in spite of mosquitoes that bit her bared skin. Darkness was her friend.

Back at the shelter, she curled into a tight ball and silently let her tears fall on the red Georgia dirt.

44

RATIONS, LICE, AND CLARA GRACE

THE GATE SWUNG OPEN, AND LONG-EARED MULES drew a wagon into the stockade. Prisoners swarmed toward the jingle of harnesses and the *clip-clop* of hooves. Rations of cornbread and bacon were doled into eager hands. Fox, Crawford, and Morgan wolfed down their bread like starved dogs on a beef carcass. A few nibbles eased Polly's hunger.

She gazed at the guard towers. Pigeon roosts, the blond man called them. She knew enemy soldiers stood there, but she didn't know who, in a Union uniform right here inside the prison, might also prove to be an enemy. She had to keep watch on the blond man, and she reckoned she needed to do it close up.

Passing rows of tents, she tried not to think about the men inside, but she couldn't help wondering how quickly she'd be able to grab the knife from her boot if she needed it. From a distance, she saw the shelter the blond man had called his shebang. He sat in the same spot as yesterday, and his fire lay as embers beneath his kettle.

She paused, took a deep breath, and sauntered right up to him. "Them coals hot enough ta cook bacon?"

"You got a stick to cook it on or you want to use my pan?"

She kept her voice friendly. "You got a pan?"

"It's half of what used to be a canteen, but it suffices." He moved his kettle off the fire, put their bacon in the canteen-pan, and settled it into the coals. He fanned the embers with his hat until they burned hot. "You want to sit?" He patted the ground beside him.

She sat, but not too close, her hand resting near her boot. Knowing that he *knew* made it hard to speak. "You been here long?"

"Thirty-three days." He pointed to tiny burn marks on a stick of pine hanging by a piece of twine from his belt. "One mark for each day. Got captured on my nineteenth birthday."

The smell of frying bacon awakened Polly's appetite. "Where ya from?" Her tone stayed as light as she could manage.

"Ohio. Near Hanging Rock. You?"

"Fowlers Gap, West Virginny." Polly scratched an itch.

"Lice?" the blond man asked.

"Reckon so." Polly looked at the tiny critter crawling in her arm hair and squished it between her thumb and forefinger. She knew lice in the ranks were commonplace. Pap had helped her keep some distance from other soldiers—and their vermin. But many hospital patients had lice. And likely men in the railroad car. Now she was in a sea of prisoners. It was bound to happen.

While they ate, the man talked about his capture. He and another soldier had been separated from their unit during a battle and had hidden from Reb patrols in a barn near Marietta.

"Barn belonged to an old woman and a girl. Their men were off fighting for the Confederacy. Clara Grace, the girl, found us. She and her granny fed us for five days. We did work around their place to repay 'em for their kindness." The man looked down and shook his head. "Their kindness got them only trouble."

"How so?"

"Rebs found us. Accused them of giving comfort to the enemy, threatened to burn their house and barn for punishment."

Polly blew out her breath. "And did they?"

"Didn't see the Rebs set the fire, but when they hauled us off, I looked back and seen smoke." He shook his head again and Polly shook hers along with him. "When I get out of this place, I'll go back to Marietta and find Clara Grace. I'll build her and her granny a new house. I ain't as strong as I used to be, but I can still do a day's work. I owe 'em. To think their men were fightin' Confederate, and Confederates burnt 'em out. Ain't fair for an army to do their own that way."

★ ★ ★

Polly lay under her lean-to shelter that night, scratching itches and thinking about the blond man. Listening to him had eased her fear—a mite. If his story about Clara Grace was true, he was a decent man. Maybe she could trust him. *If* his story was true. Maybe his friendliness had been as false as hers. She'd stay wary—and keep her knife close.

45

GRUEL

GAIN, POLLY WAITED FOR COVER OF DARKNESS to slip down to the sinks. Between sweating in the Georgia heat and rationing her clean water, she managed to have that need only once a day.

Rows of tents emitted snores and voices as she crept back. At her own shelter, she was greeted by Crawford's moaning.

"That you, Settles?" Morgan whispered. "Crawford has one hell of a bellyache, and mine's not feeling too hale, either. Fox is praying for God's healing. How's *your* belly? You ate same as us, right?"

She wondered if they had refilled their canteens from the putrid stream, but she only answered the question she was asked. "Et my bacon, but not much bread." She dug out the piece of cornbread she'd forgotten. It had crumbled inside her pouch, and she sifted the crumbs between her fingers. In the dark, she felt the difference between crumbs and tiny pieces as hard as rocks. "Feels like they ground the cob right along with the corn," she said. "Likely, cob is what's tearing up your gut."

She held Fox's head all through the night as he crumpled up in pain and tried to pray it away.

The next day, Polly stayed with her messmates until the long-eared mules brought in new slabs of cornbread. She hurried to the blond man's shebang.

"Your canteen-pan got another half somewheres?" she asked.

"I reckon it did, but I only got the one. You want to borrow it?"

"If'n ya don't mind."

She took the pan back to the lean-to and crumbled her ration of bread into it. Painstakingly, she sifted through crumbs and plucked out pieces of cob. It was a long, tedious chore, but it gave her something to do.

When she finished, she added enough water from her canteen to turn her pan of crumbs into a gruel-like mixture. Her fingers scraped it from the pan right into her mouth.

What would Miz Fletcher back home think if she saw Polly eat in this unladylike way? She almost laughed at the thought. Why, the sight of this place would probably cause Miz Fletcher to clutch her ample bosom and keel over with the faints.

After Polly had eaten, she made the same kind of gruel for Fox, Crawford, and Morgan. The pan was only large enough to do one at a time, and it took her the better part of the day.

Dusk wasn't far off when she returned the pan to the blond man. "Thank ya kindly," she told him.

"Haven't had my bacon yet. Care to join me?"

"Ain't et mine yet neither," she said.

Evening shadows crept around the campfire as they sat in silence, listening to the sizzle of bacon.

"How you manage ta stomach the cornbread they give us here? My messmates been ailin' all night and day."

"Reckon my stomach toughened up after the first week."

Polly told him how she had sifted out pieces of cob to make gruel.

"Smart girl," he said.

Polly looked at the crowd of tents close by, tents full of men whose ears might have heard that word. She jumped up and kicked the man right in his toughened-up stomach. She put her hands on her hips and looked down at him. "What did you call me?"

"Sorry," he said, when he caught his breath again. "Meant to say you're a smart feller."

She shook her fist at him. "Don't forgit it."

She watched as a smile crept around the edges of his mouth. Did he find her gender cause for a joke? Didn't he realize how dangerous her secret was? Or did he just not care?

46

PRISON LIFE

E VERY DAY WAS THE SAME. EVEN IN THE DIN OF voices, the sound of mules was like a bugle call. Cornbread and bacon. The blond man readily handed over the canteen-pan for Polly to make gruel for Fox, Crawford, Morgan, and herself. When she returned the pan, she sat with its owner while they cooked and ate bacon and talked about prison life. After dark, Polly went to the sinks.

On the third day, the men in her shelter bought a sweet potato from the sutler near the north gate. Back home, Miz Fletcher used to make sweet potatoes every year for the church supper, sweetened and seasoned until the smell of them reminded Polly of Miz Fletcher herself. She thought she'd never want to eat one again.

But this sweet potato had no spices or sweetening of any kind. It tasted only like sweet potato, and on that day, it was the best one-quarter of a sweet potato she'd ever eaten.

★ ★ ★

On her fifth day in the prison, as she waited for rations, cannon fire sounded. Fox dove for cover, while a hurry and scurry could be heard from outside the stockade walls. A battle?

Polly ducked low and slipped from tent to tent to the blond man's shebang. He always seemed to know the whys and what-fors.

"Just blank cartridges," he said. "It's their signal for an escape. Ain't heard of an escape today. I reckon this was a drill to see how quick the Reb soldiers can get to their posts."

Deep down, she had hoped to manage an escape of her own one day, but the more she saw, the more unlikely it seemed. If the blond man continued to prove trustworthy, maybe they could come up with a plan together.

A murmur of voices skimmed down the row of tents, and a cluster of men approached. A prisoner with long, stringy hair stepped out of the group and said, "We got up a petition to send to Lincoln. Ask him to exchange some of their prisoners for us."

The blond man read the petition and handed it to

Polly. "Looks like you're threatening to turn Confederate if Lincoln don't agree," he said to the stringy-haired man.

Polly looked at the petition. The words she could read were scant compared to the ones she couldn't. Reading and spelling had never come easy. She'd trust the blond man on this.

"I ain't no Reb," she said. "The Union was important to my pap—and to me. I'd jist as leave die in this devil of a place than turn Reb. I ain't goin' sign." She handed back the petition.

The petitioner sneered down at her. She crossed her arms and looked at him hard.

"Paul's right," the blond man said, standing to his full height, which was a whole head taller than the stringy-haired man. "I won't sign, either."

Until now, Polly had only seen the blond man sitting or stooped over the fire. She hadn't realized how tall he was. If she had, she might have thought twice before she'd kicked him in the stomach the other night. But he had let that kick go, when he could have easily overpowered her. And today, this giant of a man had taken her side.

He seemed honorable, but he also knew the truth about her. She wasn't ready yet for full trust.

47

HUNGER

O N HER SEVENTH DAY OF IMPRISONMENT, Polly waited and waited for the jingle of harnesses. Hunger scratched inside her belly, but the mules didn't come.

Grumbles from neighboring tents swelled with anger and frustration. When the gates opened, it was to carry out bodies. Must have been near a hundred of them. A hundred more corpses to pile in the dead house.

As she waited for rations that didn't come, Polly rolled the pebble in her pocket between her fingers. She stroked the rough side, and Pap's whiskered face seemed as near as life. She touched the smooth side, and Leander's face pleaded with her to let him help. But today he couldn't help, and neither could Pap.

What she needed was gruel and bacon. The portions

had been meager, but they had kept Polly alive for six days. And making the gruel had given her a purpose. Now she had no reason to borrow the pan, no reason to visit the blond man. She couldn't even make herself get up from the ground outside the shelter she shared with Fox, Crawford, and Morgan. Her fingers twitched, yearning for crumbs to sift through. She craved the nearly tasteless gruel like a drunk craves a nip from the bottle.

Voices from inside the shelter were like a distant drone of mosquitoes, rather than fellow prisoners who shared the same misery. Crawford played a tune on his mouth organ, but its sound fell flat on Polly's ears.

★ ★ ★

Wagons rolled through the gate at sunset—at last! Thousands of prisoners scrambled for food. Polly didn't even take time to grab her jacket as her cravings pulled her to join the rush. Her feet were kicked out from under her by the force of men. But there was no room to fall, and she was carried along for a moment without her feet even touching the ground.

Her uniform blouse was grabbed and tugged, and its buttons strained. She regained her balance and struggled to pull herself free of the crowd. With one final thrust, she pushed between two men, and one of them shoved her aside. Hard.

Pain shot through her elbow as she landed on the ground and tumbled away from the herd of feet. Her shirt had been nearly ripped off, but in the clamor, no one seemed to notice. She turned her back to the mass of men and buttoned the remaining buttons. Two were missing. Instead of leaving a gap, she buttoned her shirt crookedly, leaving a longer hem at one side, but making sure her breasts were covered. She tucked the uneven shirttails into her uniform trousers and straightened her shirt front as best she could. She returned to the shelter and put on her jacket.

Men held their rations tight against their bodies as they headed away from the food wagon, protecting their meager provisions from those who still had to wait their turns. Polly bided her time until the end of the line. She couldn't risk another near-undressing.

Dark pressed close as she toted her rations back to the shelter. Crawford had already eaten his cornbread, and Morgan chomped on cold bacon. Fox was saying grace.

Her belly was empty, but she was too tired to sift through her bread for pieces of cob, and she wasn't willing to risk stomach pain from eating it. Why was she so tired? She had done nothing all day, but she could barely lift her arms or pick up her feet.

While hunger and fatigue battled inside her and her elbow throbbed with pain, she tucked her rations in her pouch. Curling up at the shelter's edge, she gave victory to her tired side.

48

RAIN

IT WAS AFTER MIDNIGHT WHEN SHE WOKE AND MADE
her nightly trek to the sinks. The sound of the stream made
her thirsty, and when she returned to the shelter, she drank
her canteen dry. It helped fill her innards. But she had to
hurry to the sinks again before dawn, racing sunrise to
relieve herself in darkness.

Hunger stabbed through her, a pain worse than
her throbbing elbow. Crawford and Fox had the same
bellyaches as the first day.

Polly carried her canteen to the blond man's shebang.
He saw her approach and held out his pan for her to borrow.

"Ya have enough clean water ta fill my canteen? I kin
pay ya fer it." She fished in her pocket for a coin.

"What kind of man would take money from a . . ." He
looked at the way Polly's eyes narrowed. "From a friend?"

A friend. Something close to a smile tugged at her lips. "Much obliged." She shook her empty canteen. "Cain't make gruel without water."

"You didn't eat yesterday?"

She shook her head.

"Sit down," he said. "Let's have bacon first today."

While the bacon sizzled in the pan, the man filled Polly's canteen with water from his wooden pail.

"You know you're buttoned crooked, right?"

She pulled her jacket closed. "Onliest way ta keep covered on account of I'm missin' a couple buttons."

"I might have one." He dug into his pocket and sifted through an assortment of coins. "You got a needle and thread?"

Polly shook her head again.

He pulled the items from a pouch in his shebang.

"I'll bring 'em back soon's I kin," she said

That evening her gruel tasted different. The remnant of bacon grease in the pan gave it a new flavor. Or maybe going a day without it had been all the seasoning it needed.

She changed her routine. Bacon with the blond man, before making gruel for herself and her messmates. She didn't always find cob pieces in the cornbread, though she often found flies. Some routines were better unbroken.

★ ★ ★

On her ninth night of imprisonment, as Polly slipped back from her nightly visit to the sinks, she heard the growl of thunder and saw flashes of lightning above the stockade walls. A raindrop struck her cheek. And another. And another.

She walked right past the shelter where her messmates slept, and hurried through the rain to the blond man's shebang. She heard his snores as she crawled into the shelter.

"Your offer still good for me to stay here?" she whispered. He roused from sleep and murmured something she couldn't understand before he fell back to snoring.

"I hope that means yes," she said. She had to trust him now. She couldn't allow herself to get soaked again.

Rain fell harder, but the pine-bough roof kept Polly dry. She set the man's water pail outside to catch rainwater, and curled up beside him.

The rain's patter was a comforting sound, one that almost convinced her she was back home in Pap's cabin in Fowlers Gap. She even let herself believe—for just a minute—the snores she heard were Pap's.

49

BULL

"HEY!" A THROATY VOICE CALLED, ROUSING Polly awake. She sat up as a hand pulled open the shebang's blanket door, and sunlight spilled in on her and the man beside her. "Something's going on outside the camp."

The blond man sat up and rubbed his eyes. Those eyes opened quickly when he saw Polly beside him.

"It rained," she said with a shrug.

The man with the throaty voice raised his eyebrows at Polly for a second, and dismissed her with a look the next. He pulled on the blond man's arm. "There's a mess of militia stirring things up outside the southwest corner."

Polly trailed behind the two men as they headed toward the wall, where other prisoners gathered. She heard the stranger say, "You're like sweet syrup to a fly when it comes to scrawny runts. Don't you get tired of wiping noses?"

The blond man's voice was blunt. "Don't *you* get tired of picking on people smaller than you?"

The ring of axes sounded among tall pines outside the stockade. Treetops swayed and disappeared from view. Polly heard the whoosh and rustle of branches, and a loud thump as each one hit the ground.

On the rise outside the stockade, Rebs stood guard over dark-skinned men whose shovels dug in the rust-colored dirt. Other men piled the dirt and molded it into walls.

"They's building something," the stranger said.

The blond man nodded. "Earthworks. Maybe a fort. Could be the Union Army is close."

"We kin hope," Polly said.

The stranger turned to face her. "Don't think we met."

"Paul Settles," she said. "Come in nine days ago with the Army of the Potomac."

"You ain't much bigger than a louse's lap dog, Settles," the man said. "The U.S. Army must be clean out of men and boys if they're recruiting from the cradle now."

Polly doubled her fists at her sides. She didn't like this stranger and didn't care how big he was.

He took in the look on her face and laughed. "No need to punch me in the knee. I won't harm ya none." He put out his hand. "They call me Bull."

She raised her chin in defiance before she shook his hand. "Is that on account of ya smell like one?"

Bull peered down at her with a scrunched look on his face before he grinned. "Ya found one with a little fire this time, McGlade," he said to the blond man. "Not just a mama's boy."

McGlade. It was the first time she'd heard the blond man's name. She had never asked. But she knew she'd heard that name before. She didn't remember where. She'd have to think on it.

50

GOSSIP, RUMORS, AND DREAMS

THE NEW EARTHWORKS CAUSED RUMORS TO SEEP into tents and shebangs. Many believed the Rebs were building a fort because the captain feared a Union attack. Some prisoners were certain liberation was only days away.

But more prisoners arrived. More prisoners to carry in rumors and gossip. More prisoners to crowd close and fill the fetid stockade with noise and smells. And to make Polly feel more vulnerable. Thoughts of escape changed to thoughts of survival.

That night, she slept again in McGlade's shebang. She felt safer there. She still didn't remember where she'd heard his name before. Maybe at the hospital? But she couldn't recall a patient his size.

The sound of train whistles startled her awake. Common during the day, trains were unusual at night. In the darkness, a commotion stirred up among the prisoners. Scurrying, talking, speculating, carrying tales.

"More workers for the new fort."

"More Reb soldiers in case of attack."

The next morning, they saw more Negroes working outside the southwest corner. And more guards watching over them. Negro prisoners were commandeered to help. Polly watched their comings and goings with envy. Would she ever walk out those gates?

At day's end, they reported they'd dug trenches for the Rebs to fight from.

"Wouldn't need trenches unless an attack's coming," McGlade said.

"Attack or not," Polly said, "did ya notice the cornbread ration's got smaller?"

"Now they got to feed all those workers and guards, too."

As Polly sifted crumbs with her fingers, an important-looking man from the outside strolled up the street in front of her shelter. Prisoners gathered around him.

"I need recruits to fill in the swamp around the stream," he said. "Double rations for anyone who does a full day's work."

Not as good as going outside the gates to work, but Polly's stomach made her volunteer. Morgan stepped forward, too.

"I need strong backs," the man said. He pointed to Morgan and several other prisoners. He ignored Polly.

"I kin do the work," she said.

He shook his head. "Too puny."

★ ★ ★

Tales of Union troops were rampant. They were sixty miles away, according to one. Fifteen miles, reported another.

Polly didn't believe it. "Morgan says they's goin' build new sinks. Why would they need sinks if'n they think we'll git freed?"

Georgia sun blazed its heat over the camp, leaving Polly's skin sticky with sweat, sapping her strength. And withering the hopes of many.

Morgan returned from the swamp every night looking sickly. After breathing intolerable odors in oppressive heat, Polly reckoned he deserved every extra bite he was given.

★ ★ ★

Still new prisoners arrived. Rations stretched thinner. Less cornbread and no bacon at all. Rumors reported Union troops had burned food warehouses, and the prisoners had only their own countrymen to blame for their hunger.

Other gossip said a prisoner exchange would take place on August 1, just over a week away. Another rumor? And how many hundreds would die in that week? The dead already numbered nearly two hundred a day. And yet two hundred out of more than thirty thousand was hardly noticeable. Voices were just as loud, smells just as unbearable.

Flies swarmed during the day, mosquitoes at night. But the most annoying critter was hunger, always gnawing at Polly's innards, reminding her of the emptiness inside her. She held back some of her gruel until night. It eased the gnawing long enough to let her sleep.

Orders came that prisoners were not to gather in large groups near the gate. The Rebs seemed to fear an uprising. Did they truly think starving men could battle armed soldiers?

When new prisoners arrived, men surrounded them to hear news. Where were they captured? How near were their forces? Any word from outside was plucked up like a dropped crust of bread. Voices buzzed and rose and filled the camp—until a cannon's boom sounded and fired a ball just over their heads. The new men scattered. Orders were orders.

Polly was awakened by cannon fire twice that night, but she was bothered more by the emptiness in her gut. A cannonball might be easier than slow, agonizing starvation.

She dreamed about food. *Miz Fletcher cooked for her and Pap. Chicken, pork, potatoes, greens, and bread dripping with butter. As Polly reached for a knife to cut the bread, Miz Fletcher snatched it away.* The gnawing critter had crept into her sleep. Survival was going to be an agonizing battle.

51
SICKNESS

MEN FROM OUTSIDE WERE BROUGHT IN to build new sinks, and McGlade managed to latch onto a few pieces of lumber from the old ones. More firewood. He boiled water every chance he got, and generously kept Polly's canteen filled.

The gnawing critter begged her to drink it dry, to fill her innards with water, anything to put a stop to that wretched empty feeling. But work on the swamp and new sinks kept that area full of men. The thought of having to relieve herself during daylight hours made her back off and allow herself mere sips.

★　★　★

As she approached their shelter one afternoon, Morgan said, "I hardly recognize you. You're thin as a broomstick."

"So is every man in this place. I cain't remember what a full stomach feels like. Don't reckon any of us can."

"Your face is dark, too."

She scratched at her cheek. "It's from pine smoke."

"A fire in this heat? I'm ready to melt into my shoes."

She nodded. "Heat and hunger fight meaner'n Rebs."

"Sickness, too," he said. "Fox and Crawford are both ailing. It's more than cob-gut this time."

Fox burned with fever, doubled up with cramps, and could no longer control his bowels. Trying to clean him, Polly noticed blood in his stool. She recognized the symptoms. She had worked at the hospital long enough to know dysentery.

"Crawford's got it, too," Morgan said.

Polly gave them water from her canteen, water that had been boiled. She tried to make them comfortable and keep them clean. She took the last few coins from her pocket and bought an onion from the sutler. She cooked it over McGlade's fire until it was soft, and fed it to Fox and Crawford. When they would eat no more, she and Morgan shoved the rest into their mouths. She gobbled it down. It quieted the gnawing critter for a spell.

Morgan tried to help her care for the others, but he

suffered, too. His long days of working on the swamp in the heat caused him to have fits of trembling.

One day he lay down in the hot sun and didn't get up. Polly tried to pull him into the shade of their shelter, but she was no longer strong enough to move him. She mopped sweat from her face and tried again. In all that heat, Morgan's skin stayed dry. Not one drop of sweat. She held her canteen to his lips, but he wouldn't drink.

"Stay with me, Morgan," she pleaded. "They say we's goin' be swapped ta the Union. Exchange'll come August first, I hear."

★ ★ ★

The last day of July brought the threat of rain. Since Polly couldn't move Morgan, she moved their blanket-shelter to cover him. Her arms felt weak as she pounded the tent posts with a rock. In spite of their illness, Fox and Crawford crawled the few feet to its protection.

Raindrops pelted her face as Polly made certain the men were beneath the rubber blanket. She gave Fox and Crawford water from their canteens. She tried once more to coax Morgan to drink, but he lay staring, his hand over the pocket where he kept his daughter's photograph.

"Ya need anythin', Morgan?"

But he didn't speak.

Just before the rain swelled to drenching curtains, Polly hurried to McGlade's shebang, carrying with her the guilt of leaving three sick men. Maybe she should have had them taken out to the hospital, but she remembered what McGlade had said on her first day here: *The hospital is the last stop before the dead house.* Maybe they would die anyway, but it would be in the charge of someone who cared.

52

DEATH

ORNING BROUGHT SUN AND REKINDLED the heat the storm had dampened. Dripping with sweat, her uniform sticking to her skin, Polly went back to care for her messmates.

August began with no exchange and no sign of Union troops or rescue. Morgan died on the third, a day when heat seemed to seep into camp from the depths of hell. Polly tried not to think of how fierce the smell in the dead house would be.

"I'm sorry, Morgan." She struggled to keep from sobbing like a girl. Pap would expect her to be strong.

She fetched McGlade to help carry Morgan's body to the south gate to wait for the dead wagon. She removed his daughter's picture from his pocket and looked at the image of the girl who would never see her father again. Polly would write her a letter.

She searched his other pockets and found one lone coin. She slipped it in her own pocket before she removed her hat and said a few words over her him. She glanced up at the sky. "Make him welcome, Pap."

"How about I wait for the dead wagon?" McGlade offered. "You can get back to the others. I'll give them his name and particulars."

"I'm obliged," she said, as a breeze ruffled her hair and cooled her face, a welcome reprieve from the oppressive heat. For a moment, she felt it was an acknowledgment from Pap, but it only seemed Heaven-sent until she noticed clouds gathering.

"Should I expect you at my shebang at the first drop?" McGlade asked.

"Cain't leave Fox and Crawford. They'll die if'n I do. Never shoulda left Morgan. How's your boiled water holdin' out? Kin ya fill my canteen? They been emptyin' it right regular." She handed it to him.

★ ★ ★

The storm threat was only a tease. Not a drop of water, and heat returned with a vengeance. No sign of McGlade with her canteen. When a bead of sweat dripped down to her lip, her parched tongue reached out and snatched it.

Crawford moaned and called for water. Fox looked at her with glassy eyes and asked for his Bible.

How long did McGlade have to wait with Morgan's body?

As she hurried toward his shebang, gunfire sounded from a pigeon roost. Someone must have crossed the dead-line. With thirty-three thousand prisoners, it wasn't likely she'd ever met the man who was shot, but still she lowered her eyes. *How kin folks live like this, Pap? Them Rebs would as leave shoot me as not. I ain't et good in more'n a month, ain't had a bath or drawed an easy breath. This place is so full of death, I kin smell it on my own skin.*

She found McGlade stoking his fire. "I need to boil more water." He handed her the filled canteen. "This is the last I got."

It was hard to keep Crawford from drinking more than his share, but she had to save some for Fox—and for herself. Without her, they were all dead.

When she leaned down to Fox to give him his share of water, he looked up from his Bible.

"I always believed God watches over us," he said, "but He must be blind to not see what's happening here."

53

LOST DAYS

THE NEXT DAY'S CLOUDS MORE THAN THREATENED. They spat lightning while thunder boomed and rain fell with a fury. Wind snatched Polly's hat as she ran to McGlade's. She scurried to catch it and tucked it under her arm, arriving at the shebang drenched and dripping. She had no time to worry how she looked with her clothes plastered to her body. Besides, she had grown so thin she likely looked more like a boy anyhow.

"Cain't stay," she told McGlade as he filled her canteen. "Kin I borrow your water pail ta catch rain?"

He handed it to her. "Talk says an exchange is set for tomorrow."

"Don't believe a word of it," she said. "Talk's talk. Like as not, we's all gittin' outta here same way Morgan did."

For now, Fox and Crawford needed her, so she hurried

back to her shelter. Her uniform was soaked, so she sucked water from its wool sleeves, saving what was in the canteen and water pail for the others.

Rain sagged the rubber blanket until she had to push up on the sag to let it spill from the shelter like a waterfall. And still it rained. The dirt beneath her turned to mud, and the mud became puddles. She doubted there was one dry inch in all of Georgia and felt she could almost wring water out of her skin.

Low parts of the camp flooded and prisoners fled to higher ground, crowding Polly's high edge of the slope even more. She sat under the dripping blanket and watched the mass exodus. Sodden men slogged past her shelter with barely a glance, cursing the rain and the Rebs. They carried meager belongings while mud sucked at their boots, which appeared large at the ends of their scrawny limbs and gaunt bodies. Rain dripped from their hair and beards.

When the storm finally passed, the hot Georgia sun created a steamy heat that made Polly feel as boiled as water in McGlade's kettle. Strangers' tents now crowded close to the shelter where she tended Fox and Crawford. Each tent brought its own sounds to the camp's din, its own stink to the already-fouled air.

Caring for her messmates took all Polly's time. When they slept, she slept. She was so exhausted that the hunger critter couldn't keep her awake no matter how much it gnawed.

★ ★ ★

"Did you hear flood water knocked down part of the stockade wall?" McGlade said. "I heard men hauled off the logs for firewood. Wish I could've got me some of it."

Polly rarely stopped to talk. Every day was hurry-to-fetch-water, hurry-to-tend-the-sick. She lost track of days as each one seemed endless. Or did a long week just *feel* like an endless day?

She listened to Crawford gasp for air, and was certain he'd be dead before sundown. Next day he did better, and Fox labored to breathe. Polly just labored to keep up.

Gunfire was no longer a rarity. Guards in pigeon roosts enforced the dead-line more strictly. Likely to keep anyone from escaping through the hole in the stockade wall. She wondered if any crossed that line just to end their suffering.

★ ★ ★

The shelter stank from the men's waste, and Polly took to sleeping outside it, despite other tents close by. And she slept whenever time allowed, even in the hot August sun.

Her sleep flitted from nightmares of monsters who

crept in the dark, to pleasant dreams of sitting beside Leander in a cool breeze from the Coosa. But she always woke to monstrous heat, stabbing hunger, and the ever-present nightmare of prison.

During one midday nap, her hat over her face, she was roused by a sense of movement nearby. A tiny sound. A swish of dirt. A feeling of being watched. A daytime monster?

She opened her eyes, but couldn't see anything except the hat over her face. She rolled her eyes to the side to see under the edge of its brim and scanned the red dirt as best she could.

Slowly, in one smooth, unhurried motion, she slid her arm down her side. Her hand reached for the handle of the knife in her boot. Gripping her fingers around it and sliding it from its sheath, she flung off her hat.

Eyes stared at her. In one quick thrust, she flung out her hand and landed her blade.

54
THE KNIFE

"HEY, McGLADE," SHE CALLED OUT AS SHE reached his shebang. "Stoke up that fire. I brought meat." She held out her knife with the impaled lizard still flopping on her blade.

He blew on the coals and fed a small piece of wood onto them. "My firewood's about gone," he said.

While the lizard cooked, she wiped her knife blade clean on her trouser leg.

McGlade looked at it and whistled. "Mighty fine knife."

She gave a slight nod and slid the knife into its sheath, still in her boot.

The two of them ate every bite of the meat and even the skin, which had crisped over the flames. It was a small lizard, little more than a morsel. But McGlade had the fire.

He'd been good to her. It felt right to share her kill. The gnawing critter in her belly was appeased for the time being.

"This next kettle of water will be the last I can boil unless I get hold of more firewood," McGlade said. "With all the men they cook for on the outside, what firewood that comes in is scant. Digging with a tin cup for old roots ain't easy. Don't suppose you'd let me borrow that nice blade of yours? Could do some true diggin' with that."

Polly liked McGlade. And so far he'd been trustworthy. But the knife was her only chance if someone attacked her. And Pap had given her that knife. Parting with it would be like losing kin. She clung to it and didn't answer.

"If you don't trust me with it . . ."

"It ain't I don't trust ya." How could she explain what the knife meant to her? "I shared the lizard with ya."

"And I share my water with you. Been letting you fill two or three canteens at a time, but there won't be more water if I don't find more firewood. We're friends, ain't we?"

Polly clutched the knife against her chest, thinking of Pap. But she also thought of Fox and Crawford. Like as not, water from the stream had brought on their dysentery. More of it would surely kill them. They'd never survive without the boiled water McGlade provided. Would they survive anyway? Would she? What good was a knife to a dead girl?

McGlade was right. They were friends. She held out the knife by its blade and watched as he grasped its handle. No one else had touched it since Pap had given it to her.

"I promise I'll take good care of it," he said.

"If'n ya don't, I'll whup ya good, McGlade," she said, knowing full well she might not have strength enough to whup the next lizard. She turned to walk away, lest he see a tear escape.

"Hey, Paul!" he called after her. "As long as we're friends, you can call me by my front name—Given."

55

DELIVERED FROM EVIL

CRAWFORD DIED THE DAY AFTER SHE'D HANDED over her knife. She plunked his mouth organ in her pocket with the photograph of Morgan's daughter. She hadn't heard him play in quite a spell.

A couple men from the next tent helped her take his body to the gate. Other corpses lay there as though they meant no more than dead livestock. She'd wait with Crawford for the dead wagon, brushing away the flies that tried to settle on him.

After the mules pulled the wagon through the gates, she told the burial detail how to spell Crawford's name. She watched a man write it on a paper with the day's date at the top. She'd been in prison for a month now. It felt more like years.

Walking back to the shelter, she ignored the wall

of noise around her. The shuffling feet, the voices, the occasional crackle of a fire, and the wails of the hungry, the sick, and the dying had all become everyday sounds.

With only her and Fox in the blanket-shelter, the contents of four canteens lasted longer. She had no need to fetch more water from Given. She wondered if he'd found more roots with her knife. The sheath in her boot felt as empty as her belly.

★　★　★

She was at the hospital in Rome, wiping sweat from Pap's face, talking to Leander about rivers and soldiers and life. He confessed to her that he was afraid to go home, asked her if she'd go with him.

When she woke, she wiped sweat from Fox's face and helped him sit up enough to eat his share of rations. She almost heard Leander's voice, offering to help. In her dreams, Leander's face was clear. Awake, it was hard to see. She knew she should leave him in the past, but she refused. She touched the pebble in her pocket, scrunched her eyes closed, and tried harder to bring his face to her mind.

★　★　★

Fox tried to read his Bible but had trouble holding it and seeing the words.

"I ain't sure I believe anymore, Settles. The God I knew would have delivered us from this evil long ago."

Polly knew that a man's beliefs could bring him strength. She remembered a few of the Bible stories the preacher back home had told. "What about that Job feller?" she said. "With all his trials, he didn't give up on God. Ya reckon we got it worse than ol' Job?"

"Some days I think we do, but it's not right for me to question God."

"Questions ain't doubts," she said.

"Thank you, Settles, you got sense. You might not be the biggest man I ever met, but you got a bigger heart than anybody. I'd like you to have my Bible when I go."

"Don't be a-goin' nowhere jist now."

Two days later, shouts went up from the western side of the stockade wall, halfway up the northern slope. They gathered and swelled and swept through the camp. Polly couldn't leave Fox, but she knew word would carry back. Even with thirty-three thousand prisoners, gossip managed to find them all.

Like a flock of chickens at feeding time, men scurried up the street. Polly stepped out to hear the news.

"A spring!" a man cried. "There's a new spring, bubbling water cleaner than any I've seen in this place. Seems the flood dug it open. It's just beyond the dead-line, but they say it's a blessing worth getting shot for."

"Did ya hear that, Fox?" she said over her shoulder. "Clean water. I bet that's God's answer ta your prayers."

But Fox didn't hear. He'd never hear anything again.

56

REMNANTS

OLLY DROPPED TO HER KNEES BESIDE FOX'S BODY.

Why, God? He tried so hard ta believe. Ya coulda jist as leave taken me. I got no reason ta stay alive. No kin ta go home to, even if I git rescued.

She couldn't go back to Pap's cabin in Fowlers Gap. A young girl couldn't own property. Miz Fletcher might take her in, but living with that old biddy was barely a step above being dead.

In her dream, Leander had asked her to go home with him. Silly dream. What would his family say if he came home with a strange boy who was really a girl? It didn't matter. She didn't know where Leander was. She hoped he was with his family—and happy. It had been a long time since Polly had seen anyone happy.

She took down the shelter Fox, Crawford, and Morgan

had built just over a month ago. She didn't need it. She rolled Fox's body onto the rubber blanket that had sheltered them, more or less, all these weeks. The men from the next shelter helped drag the blanket to the gate.

Again, Polly waited for the dead wagon. Again, the ground was littered with lifeless, half-naked bodies, all waiting for their last ride. Many had no one to report their names to the burial detail. At least Fox had that.

As Fox's body was lifted to the wagon, she spoke to Pap. *It ain't fair, Pap, for all these men ta die so young in this miserable place. Yet I'm still here.*

She folded the blanket, adding it to her other belongings. One rubber blanket, three empty pouches, four canteens, two tent poles, a mouth organ, a tintype photograph, and one Bible. Remnants of four lives. Only her life remained. Fox had had three coins—more remnants. She dropped them into the pocket with Ma's ring and Leander's pebble.

She trudged up the northern slope to the new spring. The guards were being lenient as men ducked under the deadline to fill buckets and canteens. She filled all four canteens and headed toward Given's shebang.

The weight of four filled canteens was almost more than she could bear. Her feet dragged slowly over the ground, while dust rose around them and settled on her boots. Just over a month ago, she had marched mile after mile with the army, and now she didn't have strength enough to lift her feet.

She tried to put her mind to good thoughts. With the new spring, Given wouldn't need to boil drinking water. He could return her knife. That thought made her walk a bit faster.

As she neared his shebang, she saw Given sitting in his usual spot by the fire, but there was no fire. The ashes appeared dead and cold. He looked up and saw her, and a glimpse of a smile flickered across his face.

"I brung four full canteens from the new spring," she said. "Ya don't need ta fret about firewood no more. Look. Two fer you and two fer me." She held out a canteen.

He unfolded his legs to stand, but his knees buckled beneath him. He fell forward, knocking over his kettle and scattering ashes.

No! Not again! Not Given!

57

SCURVY

IVEN PULLED HIMSELF TO HIS KNEES AND brushed ashes from his threadbare uniform.

"Sorry," he mumbled. "My legs ain't got the strength of a fresh-hatched bird."

She dropped the canteens, knelt beside him, and helped him to a sitting position. "They bruised?" she asked. "Your limbs?"

"Some."

"Could be scurvy."

He nodded. "Likely. So tell me about this new spring."

She was certain he'd already heard about it. He always knew what went on around the camp. But if he didn't want to talk about his affliction, she wouldn't press.

He drank from the canteen she offered. "Sweetest water I tasted in a long time."

"I'm a-lookin' fer a new place ta stay," she said. "I'm the onliest one left of the three I come in with."

"Make yourself at home."

★ ★ ★

Polly trudged to the sutler's shanty near the gate. His small supply of vegetables, mostly onions and sweet potatoes, were poor quality. But she needed them for Given.

"This the best ya got?"

"Only I got. If ya wants it, best git it now afore some'un beats ya to it."

All three coins in her pocket bought only four onions and one sweet potato. She shoved them into her pockets and inside her shirt and headed back to the shebang.

The walk seemed endless as she passed bony prisoner after bony prisoner, all making do with the same skimpy rations of cornbread that had led to Given's illness. She wished she had vegetables enough to share. But there probably weren't enough in all of Georgia to feed so many.

"Where's my knife?" she asked Given, when she returned to the shebang.

"Under my bedroll."

She fetched it, taking a moment to stroke its handle and silently thank Pap for giving it to her. She sliced up an onion for her and Given. "Eat it," she said. "It'll help your scurvy."

"Don't think I can," he said, waggling a bloody tooth with his dirty finger. "They're so loose I can't chew no more."

"What about firewood? Did ya find any?"

"Couple roots yonder." He pointed just inside the shebang.

"Piece of flint?"

He pulled a small rock from his pocket.

She shaved bark from the roots and tapped her knife blade against the flint to get a spark. When the flame caught, she blew encouragement on the tiny flicker and cajoled the roots into a small fire. She fed one end of a tent pole into it as it lapped up the roots.

She poured water from a canteen into Given's kettle, and sliced the onions into it. Best to cook all of them while she had fire. By the time the flames completely devoured the tent pole, the onions had cooked down to soft bites that Given swallowed whole. She made him drink the onion broth for good measure.

When the flames burned down, she pushed the sweet potato into the coals. Something to add to tomorrow's meager gruel.

58
MAKING TRADES

POLLY SPENT MANY TOMORROWS TAKING CARE OF Given. He cried out in pain as she straightened his legs. She feared leaving them curled up too long would cause them to stay that way forever.

She'd already lost Pap. And Morgan, Crawford, and Fox. At the hospital in Rome, she'd closed the eyes of many soldiers for the last time. She refused to watch one more man die.

When the onions were gone, she went again to the sutler. Walking back to the shebang alone, with food, seemed risky among starving men. She took Given's friend, Bull, with her.

"You known McGlade long?" she asked him.

"Since our first days in the army. We fought together. And was captured together."

233

"He's powerful sick."

"Along with half this camp. Scurvy. Dysentery. And ailments I never heard of before. I keep my distance."

"I got a canteen ta trade," she told the sutler. "With the new spring, a heap o' men need somethin' ta fetch water in." She bargained him out of three onions and a sweet potato.

Instead of going back the way they'd come, Bull went to a northern area of shelters, a place the prisoners called Market Street. He handed money to a pockmarked man, who gave him a hank of tobacco and a small bottle of what looked like whiskey.

He took a quick swig from the bottle. "This is how I keep the ailments away."

★ ★ ★

Days later, a second canteen bought Polly two onions, a scrawny carrot, and a few pieces of firewood.

Given slept most of the time, once for a whole day, and she put her hand to his mouth to make sure he was still breathing. She shooed pesky flies and mosquitoes away from him when he was too weak to do it himself. She used her knife to add notches to the piece of pine he wore. She kept him clean as best she could. The new spring was a godsend.

Her days fell into a new routine. She fetched water from the spring, collected their ration of cornbread, crumbled it with her fingers to sift out flies and bits of cob, and cooked what vegetables she could get from the sutler.

Bull always went along when she fetched provisions. It was safer than walking back alone. He often stopped on Market Street to make his own deals.

She pilfered pieces of the shebang's pine-bough roof to keep her fire going. She made gruel, fed Given, ate her share. And fell into a dead sleep before the sun set. Ignoring the gnawing critter inside her had become routine as well.

In the black of night, she crept to the sinks to empty her bowels and pass what little water she hadn't sweated away in the August heat.

Bull always seemed to have a new rumor to share. But Polly no longer believed tales of Union forces on the way to rescue them.

59

SIXTEEN

POLLY'S KNIFE HAD SCRATCHED MANY MARKS ON THE piece of pine that hung from Given's belt, but she'd never bothered to tally them. After all, it was his count. By the time she did, he'd been here nearly eleven weeks.

She'd been here more than six and was well past due for her monthly lady's time. Not only did she look like a boy, but she reckoned she had become one.

★ ★ ★

The vegetables had run out again, and she was down to her last canteen. She needed it. She had already traded the other three and all three pouches. She felt Ma's ring in her pocket. Never! She would rather die.

She still had Fox's Bible. And Crawford's mouth organ.

"All the prisoners got left in this place is God," she

told the sutler. "Surely one of 'em will pay ya well fer this handsome Bible."

Three onions, two sweet potatoes, a bunch of carrots, and a speck of firewood.

Bull walked beside her toward the shebang. "An exchange is certain this time," he told her. "Next week. Word came down to be ready."

"Came down from who? There's been lies about exchanges since the day I was brung here. Ain't seen one yet."

"They say Sherman's men are close enough to smell us. It'll happen. I feel it."

"Heckfire! Smellin' us ain't no challenge. I reckon anybody with a nose kin smell us. Like as not, President Lincoln hisself, clean up in Washington, has caught our scent by now."

"You mark my words. By next week, tenth of September at the latest, we'll be heading for home."

September? When had she last counted those notches in Given's piece of pine? September had caught her unaware.

That evening, while Given slept a few feet away, she sliced a carrot into sixteen thin slices. She ate them one at a time, letting each rest a moment on her tongue before she chewed and swallowed.

She fed vegetables to Given every day but ate of them sparingly herself, to make them last as long as possible. But today was different. In her mind, she talked to Pap.

One slice fer each year, Pap. I'm sixteen now. Don't rightly know if that makes me a woman. Most days I feel more like a man. I pray that ya's helpin' me stay alive fer a reason. Might be fer this Given feller. He needs my tendin'. I'm trying ta stay strong like you woulda, but it ain't been easy.

She slowly ran her fingers along the blade of the knife Pap had given her all those years ago, and patted the pocket that held Ma's ring and Leander's pebble. A coolness enveloped her as she lay down to sleep, and her arm, curled beneath her head, felt like a soft pillow.

60
DEPARTURE

THE LATEST RUMOR CRACKLED THROUGH THE PRISON like a flame through dry brush.

"Atlanta fell!"

"Sherman took Atlanta!"

Bull hurried to the shebang. "We're movin' out. They ordered our detachment to be ready to go at first notice." He looked down at Given. "We're being exchanged."

Given struggled to raise his head. "We're getting out?"

"It's true. I told this whip of a boy five days ago it would happen, didn't I?" He looked at Polly. "Ya didn't believe me, did ya?"

Polly still wasn't sure she believed it, but she couldn't ignore the hurry and scurry in tents and shebangs close by. Prisoners gathered up what few belongings they had and talked to their neighbors about the liberation finally at hand.

Two days later, the order came for several detachments to assemble near the gate and prepare to march to the railroad depot to load onto the cars. But there was more to the order: *Able-bodied men only. All who cannot walk must remain behind.*

There was no way Given could walk on his scurvy-ridden legs, and taking care of him had become a need for Polly. At long last an exchange was happening—but she wouldn't be part of it.

"Given cain't go," she told Bull on his departure day.

"What about you? You can walk."

"He'll die without me here."

"And you'll both die if ya stay."

"I'm stayin'."

Bull shook his head. "Mule-headedness can kill ya," he said over his shoulder as he walked toward the gate.

"They'll git to us eventually," Polly promised Given, as she watched prisoners file out. "Our turn'll come. You'll see."

★ ★ ★

For three days in a row, she watched men march out that gate. Train whistles sounded throughout the day and night.

After war and battle, after starvation and sickness, soldiers were going home.

"You should go with them," Given told Polly.

"Me? Heckfire! I got no home ta go to."

"When we get outta here, I'm going back to Marietta to help Clara Grace and her granny rebuild. You can come with me."

She had nearly forgotten his vow to make things right for the women who had aided him before his capture. Did they truly want help from a Yankee who'd caused their home to be burned? And would they welcome a Yankee who brought *two* more mouths to feed?

It didn't matter. Right now he wasn't well enough to stand, much less travel or rebuild someone's home. She had listened to his moans at night whenever he moved, heard him cry out as she straightened his limbs. She had noticed the bruising along his arms and the infected mosquito bite just above his wrist. She didn't know if he'd ever be strong enough.

★ ★ ★

Polly had grown accustomed to the camp's din. After so many departures, it was almost quiet.

One day, the sound of hammering was heard from the

north edge of the prison. Long, low buildings were hastily assembled. Barracks, they were called, but they had no walls and reminded Polly of cow pens.

Men unable to walk, men with scurvy and dysentery, men with open sores and protruding bones were carried to the barracks. To Polly, it seemed like a hospital. Given had warned her: *The last stop before the dead house.*

Keeping Given out of the dead house was what kept her going. She stayed with him in the shebang, even as tents and shebangs around them were taken down or abandoned. At dusk, she scavenged through the deserted campsites. Little was left behind, but she found a couple of coins, a tin cup, and three blankets.

The night seemed large around her. She'd hated the crowded camp, where she'd heard every sneeze and moan from a neighbor, but now as the number of prisoners diminished, she felt exposed.

She watched the stars and rolled Leander's pebble between her fingers. It was warm from being in her pocket, and she let herself pretend the warmth of Leander's touch had been left behind in the stone. Her head reasoned that she'd never see him again, but her heart kept a tiny glimmer of hope alive. And that glimmer kept *her* alive.

61

THE TEMPTATION OF APPLE BUTTER

THE PRISON POLICE FORCE GOT PERMISSION TO channel the new spring away from the stockade wall, further from the dead-line. Polly could stop for a drink on her return from the sinks without fear of being shot

And with fewer prisoners, fewer guards manned the walls.

When murky moonlight eased across the dead-line's boards, Polly noticed some were loose, especially near the spring. All the leaning across and reaching under had weakened them. A quick look up to a pigeon roost, and she pulled free a board. The sound of it creaked loudly in the still night. She froze and waited, but the pigeon roosts remained silent. She pulled off another. And another. Firewood!

She stoked the fire and boiled water to soak a piece she cut from the arm of her drawers. Perhaps this ragged piece of sleeve could be used as a bandage.

The infected bite on Given's arm was red and oozed pus, but didn't smell of gangrene—yet. He had suffered three nights with chills and fever, signs she had seen often in the hospital. Those ailments had killed many, but not all. Leander had come through *his* fever. Maybe Given would get strong again, too.

★ ★ ★

As September marched closer to October, rations became more scant. Cornbread for two of them didn't fill the half-a-canteen pan. Given's bones showed through his fire-hot skin.

She returned to the sutler. "Got any stone mint? For fever?"

He shook his head.

"Jist vegetables then." She held out a spoon, all they had left besides a canteen, water pail, kettle, pan, and blankets. Crawford's mouth organ and the tin cup had been traded days ago. She refused to give up her knife or Ma's ring. And no one had use for a tintype photograph tinged green with mold. She had other plans for the coins from the abandoned tent sites.

"A spoon?" The sutler looked down his nose at her offering. "No one has anything of value left to trade. Even if someone wanted your paltry spoon, they'd have nothing to give for it."

"Your vegetables'll shrivel up and die if'n ya don't trade 'em to me. A spoon's better than nothin'."

He took her spoon and gave her a small sack of onions. "They's worth a heap more than your ol' spoon, but I'm closin' up tomorrow anyhow. No more business left in this place."

"Ya's closin'?"

"Have to. Most of my customers moved out beginning of the month. Rest of 'em ain't got shucks ta trade. Dang shame, too, seein' as I jist took in eight pint-jars of apple butter from one of the town ladies."

"Apple butter?" Polly's tongue hadn't tasted apple butter since Fowlers Gap. She'd picked apples, Pap had cooked them down, and the scent had filled half the valley. If only she could afford apple butter.

And she needed so much more than apple butter. If the sutler closed up and left, she'd have no chance to get foods to fight off Given's scurvy. But she wasn't sure Given would survive anyhow. The deep-red oozing bite on his arm had become a large pustule. If gangrene set in, there'd be no hope.

She had more to worry on than resisting the temptation of apple butter. Sweet, delicious apple butter.

"Ain't ya got somethin' better ta trade?" the sutler asked.

"Kin I see your apple butter?"

He set a jar in front of her and lifted the lid. The scent reached out and flew right up her nose, making her forget the stench that had surrounded her for nearly three months. The sweet scent of Pap and home and apple butter.

Her hand reached into her pocket, and when she held it out, Ma's ring rested on her palm.

62

GIVEN'S WOUND

THE SUTLER SUCKED AIR BETWEEN HIS TEETH AND reached for the gold circle in Polly's hand. She closed her fingers around it. It was all she had left of the ma she'd never known. She felt its shape against her skin. But the ring wasn't Ma.

The man's eyes had a hankering look. "What ya want fer it?"

Apple butter would last longer than fresh vegetables, and Given needed those things. Did she truly *need* the ring? She took a deep breath and scanned the big lean-to. "The sack of onions, them sweet potatoes, and ever' single jar of apple butter."

"Done," he said.

"And that whetstone."

He reached it down and set it on his table.

"If ya ain't got nothin' fer fever, ya got any woundwort?"

He shook his head.

"Gumweed? Coltsfoot? Yarrow?"

"Sorry, no."

"How's about somethin' fer a burn?"

"You got a burn?"

"Ain't fer me."

"Got some patent salve that's s'posed to be good on burns."

"I'll take it. And a box ta tote it all in."

"Deal."

"And my spoon back. If ya fetch it all ta my shebang in an hour, I'll give ya the ring." She gave him directions.

What would Pap think about her trading away Ma's ring? She didn't have time to listen for his scolding voice in her head. She had too much to do.

Her next stop was Market Street, where she looked for the pockmarked man Bull had made trades with. The street was near empty now, and likely the man had left with Bull and the others.

When a man walked past her, she caught the smell of whiskey on his breath.

She grabbed his sleeve. "Kin ya tell me where ta find a drink?"

The man drew a bottle from his pocket. "Ya got money?"

She reached the coins from her pocket that she'd found in deserted tent sites. The man grabbed them eagerly.

★ ★ ★

With the bottle of whiskey safely tucked under her bedroll, she watched as the sutler lugged the box down the street.

He set it outside the shebang, and she looked through it before she handed over Ma's ring. Her pocket felt achingly light as she watched him walk away. *Sorry, Pap, but a ring won't keep nobody alive.*

She unloaded the items inside the shebang and broke up the wooden box to stoke her fire. She poured water into the kettle and set it on the flames.

As fire lapped at the bottom of the kettle, she opened a jar of apple butter and spooned a taste onto her tongue. She let the smooth sweetness fill her mouth for several seconds before she swallowed. The taste remained on her tongue, but her stomach begged for more. She ate another spoonful. And another.

By the time the water boiled in the kettle, she was scraping the last bite of apple butter from the bottom of the jar. Her stomach had gone from hungry to content to complaining.

She hurried behind the shebang and heaved it up.

When she finished retching, she wiped her face on her sleeve and remembered what the sutler had said. *Apple butter from one of the town ladies.* A Southern lady. A Rebel lady. Did that lady know it would be sold to a Yankee prisoner? Was it poisoned? Or had Polly just forced more down her gullet than her half-starved stomach could handle?

She took a drink from her canteen and gave her stomach a few minutes to settle. The sick feeling left her. After parting with Ma's ring to buy the apple butter, she chose to believe it was safe to eat. She just needed to take it in smaller doses.

Right now, more important things were on her mind. The water was ready. She put used-to-be-drawers bandages in the boiled water to soak.

She opened the bottle of whiskey. "I got medicine fer ya, Given."

He groaned as she lifted his head, the heat from his fever seeping through her sleeve.

"Ya got ta drink this."

He drank a few swallows and turned his head.

"Ya's goin' need more'n that," she told him and tipped up the bottle again.

She didn't stop coaxing until the bottle was half empty.

His head fell back, and she hoped he had passed out.

After sharpening her knife on the whetstone, she tried to get him to take another drink, but he was unconscious. Good. It was better that way.

Wiping the blade of her knife with a boiled bandage, she cleaned it until she could see her face in its blade. She held Given's arm beneath the weight of her boot and plunged the knife's tip into his skin.

He yelped and flailed, but her boot held his arm fast and he was too weak to fight. With quick, sure strokes, she cut around the pustule and flung it out of his skin. Blood streamed from the open wound. Ignoring the heat's assault on her hand, she held the knife blade in the flames. In one quick motion, she pulled Given's skin over the wound and laid the hot blade across it. The smell of burnt flesh pierced the air along with Given's scream.

But the bleeding stopped.

63
MOVING

GIVEN BLAZED WITH FEVER FOR FOUR DAYS, and Polly fed him water laced with whiskey. He thrashed around in his sleep and called out, sometimes for his ma, sometimes for the girl named Clara Grace. She hoped he'd live to see them both again.

Watching his feverish fits made Polly remember when she'd first seen Leander. Even if she survived the ordeal of prison, she knew she'd likely not see him again. Still, she held that glimmer of hope inside her.

She checked Given's burn throughout each day, looking for signs of infection, but found none. She straightened his legs when he curled them, and it didn't seem to pain him as much as before. But that might have been from the whiskey.

As she moved about, caring for him, she was aware of the silence in her pocket. She had gotten used to the *clink* of Ma's ring against Leander's pebble. Now, she found herself touching her pocket to make sure the pebble was still there.

When Given's fever broke and he opened his eyes, he saw the burn on his arm. He looked up at Polly and said with a croak, "What happened?"

"Ya was fever-y from a skeeter bite what got infected. But it's gone. Ya's better now."

"And the scurvy?"

"No worse."

"We got any food? I'm hungry."

"Right glad ta hear it. Ya like apple butter?"

One October day, word came that the Reb captain wanted to separate the sick from the healthy—not that *any* of the prisoners were healthy. Those not in the hospital barracks on the northern slope were to be marched to the south end of the camp.

Polly took down and folded the blankets that made up the sides of the shebang. She removed its pine-bough roof and laid it in one piece on the rubber blanket from her old shelter. She set their few belongings atop that, sliding the last of the food into the kettle. She slipped her canteen strap over her shoulder.

Given had gotten stronger, but he still hadn't been able to stand, much less walk.

"Ya gotta walk," Polly told him. "Otherwise, they's goin' put ya in the hospital sheds."

"No hospital," he insisted. "Might as well be dead."

"Then ya gotta stand." She pulled on his arm and helped him to his feet. He wobbled and leaned heavily on her shoulders.

"I'll tug the blanket behind us," she said. "Lean your hand on my shoulder and hold onto the blanket so's it looks like ya's helpin' me. Don't let 'em see ya's weak. It's mostly downhill. Ya kin do it." She wasn't sure he could, but she knew he had to.

At a turtle's pace, they trudged down the slope to the stinking creek and crossed the bridge. Slowly, slowly, plodding one step at a time, making the load appear heavier than it was—though it was far from light.

Given's step faltered, and the weight of his hand grew heavy. She stopped and turned as if to check the load. When he had steadied himself enough to walk again, they continued up the other side.

The captain reorganized these prisoners into detachments of five hundred, squads of one hundred, and messes of twenty-five. He instructed them to rebuild their shelters on this sandy spot south of the creek. He ordered straight lines on regular streets. And he warned them they'd be in this spot all winter.

All winter? Could Given survive the whole winter here? Could she? Were rescue rumors truly only rumors? Had the Union Army forgotten them all?

64

WINTER WEATHER

THE STINK WAS STRONGER IN THIS SPOT, CLOSE TO the creek. And setting the shebang's posts was a struggle. Sand filled the holes as quickly as Polly's fingers dug them. She poured water from the canteen to make it firm.

"Like as not," she said, "they moved us here on account of there's no way ta dig a tunnel." She set the poles deep, and the shebang roof rested just above Given's head when he sat up.

He sat up more as days passed. He uncurled his own legs and was able to tend the fire. Polly fetched rations and water.

When the weather turned cold and rainy, keeping a fire going was impossible. Inside the shebang, Polly dug a furrow and lined it with the rubber blanket. Under their other blankets, she and Given slept against each other to share body warmth during bitter cold nights. Some nights, she wrapped him in blankets and slept on top of them to keep him from catching a chill, ever fearful his fever would return.

Near the end of October, Rebs moved out three detachments of prisoners. More exchanges, they said. Polly stayed. She knew Given could never survive a long trip.

More than eight hundred prisoners marched out two weeks later, leaving only about two hundred on the creek's south side. Days later, they moved out some of the sick from the hospital.

"We should go with them," Given said.

"How far ya think you'll get on them bent limbs of yours? And do ya trust Rebs who barely feed us? I say we stay put."

A Reb officer came past the remaining shelters, looking for able-bodied men. "We want fightin' men," he said, "willin' to pledge an oath ta the Confederacy."

"Never," Polly vowed. "I'll never turn Reb."

After several of their number marched away with the Reb officer, Given let loose a string of swear words. "We're making a mistake," he said. "Those Reb recruits will get fed decent so they're up to fighting."

"Fightin' who? More of us, that's who. You want ta fight

our own jist ta git a decent meal? I'd as leave die here."

"And you just might," Given said.

"But I'd die loyal." If only she felt as brave as her talk.

★ ★ ★

Icy air seeped into the shebang, and Polly built a fire whenever she got her hands on wood—hands that shook in the cold as she lit the first spark. She and Given spent their days so close to the fire its smoke stung their eyes. They spent nights huddled together for warmth.

As December blew in colder than November with still more rain, they stayed in the shebang, leaning against each other.

Talking helped pass minutes that seemed as long as hours. Polly hadn't talked much since she'd joined the army, letting silence guard her secret. But Given already knew her secret.

They talked about summer, hoping for a bit of warmth in a remembered sunny day. Polly told Given about Pap and Fowlers Gap. Given talked about summers in Ohio and his pa, who made shoes.

"He drove his cobbler's wagon all over the county," he said. "I took care of Ma and Lila."

"Who's Lila?"

"My sister."

Leander had talked about a Lila, too. But Polly didn't mention that other Lila. Thoughts of Leander were sweet sadness.

★ ★ ★

When Polly left the shebang to gather their day's rations, each breath hung like steam in front of her. She cupped her hands over her mouth and nose in hopes of catching some warmth—but cold was all she felt.

The vegetables were long gone, and the last apple butter had been eaten a week ago. Those foods had helped Given fight off the scurvy. But now cornbread gruel was the usual meal, with an occasional bite of meat.

According to the scratches on Given's piece of pine, Polly had been in Andersonville prison for more than five months. It was nearly Christmas. She had dreams of Christmases back home. Pap always had a surprise for her on Christmas morning. The knife in her boot was from when she was eleven. And there had been candy. Polly tried to remember the taste of candy, but all her tongue could recollect was gruel.

A few days before Christmas, Rebs marched a thousand new prisoners into camp in a driving rain, but no new shelters went up on the sandy soil. These prisoners had no tents or blankets. They sat with their legs drawn up to their

259

chests and shivered as rain drenched them.

Polly looked out from the shebang. "It don't seem right fer us ta have shelter and them not. But how kin I let men git close . . . and . . . and still have my . . . privacy?"

"I can put myself between you and them," Given said. "And we can let 'em know right off it's just till the rain quits."

They squeezed four men into the shebang, until it was tight as peel on apples. The six of them would have to sleep sitting up. But the warmth from more bodies would make sleep easier.

The new men settled themselves into the damp sand, the smell of wet wool uniforms filling the shelter.

A hand yanked back the blanket door, and a face appeared in the opening. A throaty voice hailed a greeting. It was Bull.

65
POLLY'S DECISION

"BULL!" GIVEN CALLED OUT. "YOU WAS EXCHANGED months ago. I expected you'd spend Christmas in Ohio."

Rain dripped off Bull's nose. "Wasn't no exchange. All they done was haul us off to another prison in east Georgia. Sherman's boys got too close, so they hauled us back here. The rumors of Sherman taking Atlanta were true. He burned 'er to the ground before he left. Seen it on our way through."

"What about us?" Polly asked.

"Wish I could say, Settles. Nobody seems to care we're here—if they even know about us. Best we can do is stay alive until we can't no more. Ya got room under your roof for me? After all, I'm an old friend. Right, McGlade?"

Polly remembered how Bull had left when Given was

sick, without a thought to whether he lived or died. What kind of friend did that?

"Sorry," she said. "There ain't room for one more bean in this can."

★ ★ ★

And tinned beans were a rare treat with their Christmas dinner. The day after was cornbread again. Given had come through the worst of the scurvy and was getting stronger every day, but Polly worried he'd fall sick again with nothing but gruel to eat.

The day after Christmas saw more prisoners brought into camp, more prisoners to shiver through a Georgia winter, more prisoners to share the meager rations. Some had tents or blankets. When the rain finally backed off, they threw together shelters, and Given and Polly had their shebang to themselves again. Bull became a frequent visitor.

Late January brought another cold rain that lasted four days. Polly felt soaked clean to the marrow of her bones. And bones were about all her skinny body had left.

★ ★ ★

Early in February, a Reb colonel came into the camp to sign up recruits to fight with Confederate troops.

"With a Reb uniform," Given told Polly, "I could find

Clara Grace without some Southerner shooting me for being a Yankee."

"What if ya cain't find her?"

"I'll start where I last saw her. If she ain't there, I'll just keep looking." At least he had a place to start. Polly didn't know where to begin to look for Leander.

"We don't truly need to *fight* Reb," Given said. "We'll sign up, get a few meals in our bellies, and light out first chance."

Polly shook her head. She had managed to keep her secret in this prison. What chance would she have in a new army with new soldiers to fool? As bad as it was, she knew she had to stay.

"I won't turn Reb, not even fer show. Pap wouldn't like it. What will your kin in Ohio say if'n ya turn Reb? Don't reckon they'd like it anymore than Pap would."

Pain twisted Given's face. "I'll hope they don't find out."

"Best stay here and not have the worry."

"But we'll starve to death if we stay here."

"And who's starvin' us? Ya aim to be one of *them?*" But even as she spoke, she saw how gaunt Given's face had become. He was already near-starved.

"I need to get back to Clara Grace, whatever way I can,"

Given said. "She lost everything for helping me. I owe you for taking care of me, but now I got to take care of *her*. We need to sign up with Colonel O'Neil. He marches out in the morning."

Polly didn't sleep. She took her nightly trek to the sinks and walked slowly back to the shebang. Lack of proper food would surely bring on Given's scurvy again, even if he didn't starve to death. Going with the colonel might be best for him. But it would never be right for Polly. She hated the thought of staying behind without him, but she had to let him go. She had kept him alive. Now she had to give him a chance to *stay* alive.

66

A NEW PAUL

"PAUL SETTLES SHOULD SIGN UP WITH COLONEL O'NEIL,"
Polly told Given the next morning.

"Good, you're coming with me."

"I'm stayin', but you kin sign on as Paul Settles. After
all, Paul ain't no flesh-and-bone person. Jist a name me and
Pap made up. It don't matter if'n he turns Reb. Your kin
won't know it's you, and Pap's in a place where he'll know it
ain't me. His thinkin' is the onliest I care about."

"What about you? You won't go with me?"

"I'll stay here and be Given McGlade. If'n them rumors
ever turn true fer exchange, that'll be *my* name."

Given grinned. "Yes, yes. When you get exchanged,
you can go to Ohio, to my house. Ma'll take you in. You
can tell her why I had to do what I have to do."

The idea caught fire in both of them, and Given spilled

over with details about his home in Ohio, telling her about the new person she was about to become. He removed the piece of pine from his belt and handed it to her. "So you can keep track of days," he said. "All but thirty-two of them marks are yours as well as mine."

"Good luck ta ya, Paul Settles," she said.

"Be strong, Given McGlade," he told her. "I owe you my life. You're a strong man, for a you-know-what."

She watched Given fall into line with the other soon-to-be Rebs. He was so much taller than the rest. He looked back over their heads and gave her a weak smile. She hoped he would find his Clara Grace, and that she would welcome him.

Bull stood beside her. "They tricked me once," he said. "Hope he knows what he's doin'." Bull walked away, leaving Polly to watch Given march out the gate with the Reb colonel.

"I hope so, too," she said to the empty place inside her. So many partings this past year made her heart feel more hollow than her belly. She wiped tears on her sleeve and walked back to the shebang, clutching the pebble in her pocket.

Making gruel, fetching water, taking care of Crawford, Morgan, Fox, and Given had demanded Polly stay alive.

She didn't know if she could survive without them. She thought about helping to look after the sick in the hospital sheds, but she couldn't do it. She couldn't bear to watch one more man die.

Each day became an endless chore of getting through to the next endless day. Her skin hung on her bones like gooseflesh with no goose beneath it. Her fingers could wrap clean around her upper arms and touch on the other side.

She shivered through nights alone in the shebang, trying to latch onto a good dream. She wrapped her arms around herself for warmth, wishing for Leander's one-armed hug instead. The cold seeped so deep into her innards she couldn't feel the glimmer of hope anymore.

Every morning, she woke with surprise that she wasn't dead yet.

67

FRESH AIR

EBRUARY PASSED AWAY IN AGONY AND MARCH LIMPED in without hope. Days crawled like the lice on Polly's skin and in her hair.

Rumors came and went. Sherman's troops had moved into South Carolina and Lee's Rebs were on the run. Was Given still a Reb? Were the rumors even true?

In the prison, life stayed the same—except for those who died. Bodies were carried out to the burying trench every day. Polly reckoned one day it would be her turn. When it happened, would someone notice she wasn't like the others?

Her uniform was threadbare and she struggled to keep her skinny self covered. She made gruel each day, and once in a great while, the prisoners were given chunks of beef. Polly ate it raw.

She slept in the sandy furrow she had made for her and Given. Where did he sleep now? Was he somewhere warm? Was he eating well? Had he found Clara Grace? He often visited her dreams, as did Leander. She wondered if either of them ever thought of her.

Waves of regret overtook her when she thought of Leander. Why hadn't she stayed in Rome? But if she had, likely Given wouldn't have pulled through the scurvy or staved off gangrene. He'd have died without her. She knew that. But what had happened to him after he left? She had to believe he was still alive.

Every day she scratched another mark in Given's piece of pine. She made them smaller because she was running out of room. And she spent hours rolling Leander's pebble between her fingers.

It was mid-March when exchange rumors reached into the prison with a new fury. It was certain this time, Bull said.

"Ya said that last time," Polly said. "How kin ya believe it again?"

"This is different," he said. "I can feel it."

Polly made her gruel and tried not to get her hopes up, but two days later they were ordered to line up at the gate.

Remembering when Bull and other prisoners had

returned without so much as a blanket, she wrapped a blanket around her shoulders. At the spring, she filled her canteen so full she couldn't fit the cork into it. She took a swig and tried again. Before sliding the piece of pine with its burn marks and scratches into her waistband, she made sure Leander's pebble was safe in her pocket.

Joining the line near the gate, she looked at the men around her. The only name she knew was Bull's. Since Given had left, she'd kept to herself and waited to die. She hadn't wanted to make a friendship or care about anyone, only to end up separated by distance or death. Being alone would be her life from now on.

The line of prisoners marched through the inner and outer gates. Polly turned to see the last gate behind her. She was outside the stockade! A quivery feeling crept up her legs to the piece of pine in her waistband. She had counted its marks the night before. Now she stepped beyond those gates for the first time in two hundred fifty-one days.

She looked northward to the burial trenches. Thousands of dead prisoners had been carted to that place. How many would be forever forgotten? She thought of Fox, Crawford, and Morgan, and promised to remember them always.

The prisoners marched along a line of pine and scrub oak, stunted oaks struggling for life beneath their own pine prison. Polly had seen the tops of those pines every day, but now she took her first deep breath in a very long time. The fragrance of pine rushed inside her nose. She breathed it in again and again. The prison stink was gone. At last!

The men around her gave a cheer. Bull clapped her on the back. But Polly was wary. Was it truly over?

68

THE JOURNEY

THE SUN SHIMMERED ABOVE THE PRISONERS AS they marched to the railroad depot, where a train sat at the platform, its chimney belching smoke. The sun felt warm on Polly's skin, but it never reached the chill in her bones. She struggled to spark a glimmer of hope in the cold emptiness within her. But even outside prison walls, the future staring at her seemed bleak. What could an orphan girl with no kin and no friends do?

Might be Leander was still at the hospital in Rome. He *had* been reluctant to leave. Might be he was helping tend patients. He *had* always tried to help her do it.

She climbed into a cattle car and claimed a spot in the corner. The whistle blew, and the train pulled from the station. Andersonville was behind her. She didn't look back.

She peered trough the car's slats as the train rattled through Georgia and into Alabama.

Once Georgia was behind, she knew she was getting farther from Rome. But this wasn't the time to look for Leander. She was Given McGlade now. She couldn't be a deserter with his name. And she had to find his folks to tell them what he'd done and why.

The prisoners climbed down at a station beside a river, where they were given soup, milk, and tea. Polly ate sparingly, remembering the apple butter that had made her sick all those months ago. The soup warmed her belly, but it didn't reach her cold bones. Bad memories gnawed at her soul, and she tried to recollect the few good ones she had stored away. But even the good ones had tinges of loss tacked onto the ends of them.

The journey went on, day after day, as they were moved onto boats to cross rivers and loaded back into railcars on the other side. Most stops included a bite to eat, and Polly's empty belly welcomed every morsel.

She tried to read signs as they passed through each town. Selma. Demopolis. She didn't know how to say the words they spelled, but each one put Andersonville farther behind.

Injury and disease traveled with them. At each depot,

the dead were removed from the train. Many Union soldiers had reached their final stop.

More signs. Meridian. Jackson.

At Jackson, they left the train to resume the journey on foot. Step after step, mile after mile, Polly trekked across Mississippi. Her boots chafed, but she carried memories that weren't all bad. Her knife made her think of Pap. The piece of pine in her waistband reminded her of Given. And in her pocket, she still had Leander's pebble.

Several prisoners fell dead during the march, and their bodies were loaded onto wagons to be buried in the nearest town.

Death had become the usual. It was expected. After all the trials these men had suffered—and survived—in Andersonville's prison, death snatched their last breath in another Southern town.

69

CAMP FISK

THE MARCH TOOK THEM ACROSS A PONTOON bridge.

"The Big Black River," one man said. "We ain't far from Vicksburg." Last Polly had heard, Vicksburg was in Union hands. No rumor had said otherwise.

Nearby, homes sat in ruins. The war had been brutal here.

They marched into a tent city, a place called Camp Fisk. They were told it was a neutral site, but the flag that flew from a post bore the stars and stripes, and their captors released them into Union hands.

Released! At last! Men shouted and danced as their Reb captors departed. Polly merely sat on the ground and clenched fistfuls of earth. Union soil.

The soldiers, no longer prisoners, were given new uniforms and an opportunity to bathe. Polly waited outside the tent where tubs and buckets of water beckoned her to rid herself of the smell she had carried across three states.

A man gave her a jar of a brownish mixture. "This'll get rid of your lice and their nits," he said. "Throw your old uniform on that pile, so we can burn it. Throw that blanket there, too."

She waited until all the other men were finished in the bath tent. She carried her new uniform inside, and she hurriedly scrubbed her hair and skin with the jar's mixture. She wished she had scissors to cut her hair. It had grown quite long during her imprisonment. But many of the men had long hair, too.

Several gathered by the fire where their old uniforms were set ablaze. Even in new uniforms, the former prisoners were easy to tell apart from Camp Fisk soldiers. It was like the difference between scrawny, plucked chickens and well-fed geese.

Polly watched as flames consumed remnants of that place that had ended thousands of lives and killed a part of her as well. She held the piece of pine whose burns and scratches marked her two hundred fifty-one days, and thought about tossing it in the fire. Watching it burn might finally warm her to the bone.

But she couldn't do it. Most of those days belonged to both her and Given. Somehow, holding onto it gave her hope that he was still alive.

The released men were given hardtack. Polly recollected when she'd grown tired of it, before her capture had limited her meals to gruel. It wasn't near as tasteless as she remembered.

She borrowed paper and wrote letters to the kin of Fox, Crawford, and Morgan, telling them their soldiers died brave but not spelling out their suffering. She included the photograph of Morgan's daughter with his, giving one last look to the girl who, like her, no longer had a father.

Camp Fisk became her new home, and spring settled in around it. Dogwoods bloomed in a show of life that defied the existence of war and death.

And when word came of another demise, it was the death of the war itself. A message reached Camp Fisk that General Lee had surrendered more than a week ago. The long, bloody war was over.

A celebration erupted at Camp Fisk. She watched as Bull celebrated with soldiers and former prisoners. They were drinking hard and she stayed clear. She needed to avoid the only man who knew her name was not Given McGlade.

She tried to summon the joy she witnessed in the men around her. But with no war, her value as a soldier would shrivel like an old potato. And the house-turned-hospital in Rome would go back to being a house. If there had been a sliver of hope that she could return and find Leander, that hope had died, too.

70

VICKSBURG

SUNSHINE BEAMED DOWN ON POLLY AND THE other former prisoners as they prepared to board a train for Vicksburg. It was an April Sunday, and the men were jubilant. They were headed home—at least, the ones who had homes to go to.

As they lined up to board, a man waited with a ledger. It reminded Polly of her arrival at Andersonville, and a chill gripped her, a chill she had carried inside her all winter long. The spring thaw had never reached her innards.

Bull fell into step beside her. *Not now!* What would he do when he heard her claim her name was Given McGlade?

She said the name quietly, but the man with the ledger made her repeat it. "Given McGlade," she said louder.

Bull looked at her, his eyes wide, but he said nothing.

"I'm obliged," she said as they climbed onto the train, "that ya didn't dispute my name."

"I don't care who you claim to be," he said. "I'm going home."

Home, Polly thought. Would she ever have one again?

* ★ ★

The cars carried them past swamps and into ruined land, land defiled by war. The war was over, but the suffering here continued. Polly wondered if Bull's home would be the same as when he left.

The train pulled into Vicksburg, a city that sat on a bluff overlooking a bend in the river.

An American flag flying from a building caught Polly's eye. General Grant had taken Vicksburg nearly two years ago. Had its people become resigned to Union control? Was this Southern town as joyous that the war was over as the men who arrived on the train?

The former prisoners marched to the busy, boisterous waterfront. Men lifting and toting, shouting and hurrying, while tall stacks of boats towered above the clamor.

Polly's mind went to Pap. Pap had always loved rivers, and this one was wider and wilder than any she had ever seen. The Mississippi. Its water surged past, powerful and alive. She wished Pap were here to see it.

Following orders, she joined a long line to board one of the steamboats. The line wound around itself over and over again.

As she waited her turn, a murmur began at the front of the line and crackled along from man to man. Shrieks and groans rose from the soldiers before they passed the word down the line.

"Somethin's wrong," she said to Bull. "Might be they won't let us board."

"I'll find out."

He slipped from the line and snaked his way toward the front of it. She watched him stop to talk with a man who cried unashamedly.

Bull returned to Polly. "Lincoln's dead," he said. "Shot last week. Even though the war was already over."

Death no longer stunned her. Since Pap had died, loss was no stranger. Fox, Crawford, and Morgan were gone. And all those bodies tossed on the dead wagon. She added President Lincoln's name to a very long list inside her heart. She waited for tears to come, but her eyes stayed dry. She had learned to keep those feminine feelings in hand.

★ ★ ★

As Polly stood in line, she watched men load cargo onto the steamboat. Crates of wine, barrels of sugar, horses, mules, hogs.

And soldiers.

As the boat's decks filled, she watched crew members shore up sagging upper decks with additional posts. And more men boarded. Polly feared there wouldn't be enough room for her.

71
THE SULTANA

AS THE BOARDING LINE INCHED ALONG THE dock, Polly's eyes took in the steamboat with her decks rising above the water, her two smokestacks towering higher still. She was a side-wheeler, her name painted in tall letters on her hull.

"How ya say 'er name?" she asked Bull.

"*Sultana.*"

"*Sultana,*" she repeated.

The line of men stopped and waited as ladies, children, and gentlemen boarded. Most disappeared inside the boat's cabins, away from the press of men along the decks.

Polly wondered how long the trip was to Ohio's Camp Chase, where she, as Given McGlade, would be mustered out from the army. She'd travel up the Ohio River to the place near Hanging Rock to find Given's folks. She'd tell them about his plan to escape from the Rebs and find Clara Grace. She had promised him.

But what if he hadn't escaped? Had the Union captured him as a Reb soldier? Or shot him in battle? With the war over, had the Rebs freed him? She hoped he'd escaped long ago.

After she delivered his message, what then? What future awaited an orphan girl who'd lived two years as a soldier? Might be she should stay a boy and look for work.

She'd worry on that later. First she had a promise to keep.

Men filled all three decks of the *Sultana*, standing at the rail closer together than pine needles on a tree. And more men stood on the roof. But no one stopped Polly from walking across the gangplank and squeezing into their number. She snaked her way toward the bow of the lower deck, the one called promenade deck.

Looking toward the dock, she saw a long line of men still waiting. She was relieved to have boarded before they turned the rest away. And surely that moment was at hand.

But men continued to walk the gangplank, continued to wedge themselves among others on deck.

Polly sat against the rail, drawing her knees tight against her chest. The constant trudge of feet swayed the boat, and the *Sultana's* occasional thump against the wharf boat drowned out the lap of water against the hull. Polly breathed in the scent of river water, grateful for any smell that wasn't Andersonville.

She watched the men around her, men who had suffered the hell of battle and prison: starvation, deprivation, and disease. Yet, they had survived and now rejoiced to be heading home. She closed her eyes and leaned forward on her arms, hoping to sleep, hoping to find Leander in a dream.

It was nearly dark when Polly woke to sounds louder than men close by. A thunder of footsteps from the gangplank announced the arrival of more troops. The deck was already so crowded Polly couldn't imagine where they would go. But they were pushed and squashed into spaces that hadn't seemed like spaces a moment ago.

After dark, the *Sultana* pulled away from the dock. The boat moved slowly under the weight of so many. Polly slept as best she could with men pressed close around her. She curled up to protect herself.

In the morning, food was passed hand to hand. She stayed in her spot near the bow and accepted what was offered. Hardtack. After surviving the gnawing hunger critter in Andersonville, no food tasted bad. She smelled coffee, but none was passed to her. She still had water in her canteen, and she washed down the hardtack with swigs from it. But not too much. She'd have to squeeze through all the men to use the boat's water closets.

Polly watched the shore with its houses and farms. She watched the river with its boats and debris. The water stretched wide, and Polly reckoned the river had seen a recent flood. Now and again, a floating branch struck the bow below her place at the rail. But the boat kept chugging upriver.

★ ★ ★

On the second morning, the *Sultana* neared a port. Other passengers said it was Helena, Arkansas. Helena's townsfolk gathered on the riverfront to watch the boat. A photographer stood on the riverbank, his camera set up on its skinny legs.

"We's goin' get our picture took," shouted a man on board.

A sudden rush to the port side caused the boat to list, dipping that side near to river level. Polly wrapped her arms around the railing in fear they would capsize.

72
COLD AND DARK

THE PASSENGERS MOVED BACK TO THEIR PLACES, and the *Sultana* righted just in time. Polly breathed easier, but kept her grip on the rail until the boat docked securely.

They remained in port a mere hour before the steamboat chugged away from Helena, slowly resuming its northward journey.

A group of religious ladies led the passengers in hymns, and some of the men sang along. When they sang "Amazing Grace," Polly could almost hear Pap's deep bass. Missing him threatened to choke her.

★ ★ ★

Their next port was Memphis, Tennessee, a good-sized city where Polly watched men offload hogs, wine, and sugar. A number of passengers disembarked to find a tavern or a church, a drink or a hot meal.

Those departures gave Polly room to uncurl her legs, to move around. She made her way to the water closets. It was much easier than last night when she'd wedged through the throng of men, using her arms like a swimmer to make a path for herself. She was grateful her ordeal at Andersonville had taught her to hold her bladder for long stretches of time.

An orange sunset turned a passing boat's wake into bright streams. Polly admired its beauty and remembered other sunsets. She thought of the Coosa and Leander, of home and Pap. But the sun disappeared and renewed the chill that had taken up residence inside her. She was alone, even among the many.

"Hey, Settles!" Bull called out.

"McGlade," she corrected.

"No matter. There's open space on the boiler deck. It's warmer there."

Warmth was a true temptation, but Polly reckoned plenty of men would have the same thought. She'd stay in her spot on the bow, as separate from men as possible. Pap had warned her.

"You go ahead on. I'm fine as a flea's eyelash right here."

The bell on the *Sultana's* hurricane deck announced impending departure, and jolted Polly awake. She shook loose the cobwebs of a dream. She'd been back in the prison, freezing inside the shebang, begging Given not to die.

She took a deep breath and touched the piece of pine in her waistband. Given was alive somewhere. He had to be. She refused to give credence to one more death.

The *Sultana* chugged away from Memphis and crossed the river to a coal yard on the Arkansas side. Lights from the shore and the boat outlined men who heaved bushels of coal on board. The *Sultana* seemed to groan beneath the added weight.

★ ★ ★

In the dark night, the *Sultana* pulled away from the Arkansas shore. Again, Polly tried to dispel the chill that gripped her, at least long enough to fall sleep. When she awoke, she'd be closer to Ohio.

Dreams enveloped her again. *She trudged from the sinks at Andersonville, but couldn't find the shebang in the dark. She drew close to the new fort, where cannons stood on the hillside outside the stockade. She crept low to the ground.*

She saw the shebang, but when she got close, it was gone. Where was Given? Just as she saw his face, it wasn't Given, but Pap.

She called to him, but he didn't hear. She couldn't reach him. And blackness closed around her.

KER-BOOM! Cannon fire! A huge cannon! A cannonball struck and flung her through the air until she plummeted into icy water.

The frigid water jolted her awake. She was underwater, cold water. She couldn't breathe, and she was about to drown. Truly drown. No dream. She heard Pap's voice calling to her.

73
MORE DEATH

ICY WATER SAPPED HER MEAGER STRENGTH. SHE WAS tired of fighting, tired of the struggle to stay alive. It would be easy just to let the Mississippi take her. Maybe it was time to quit.

Pap's voice called to her again. She tried to believe he wanted her to come to him, but she knew better. She knew he was scolding her to not give up. She still had to find Given's kin and tell them he hadn't truly turned Reb. She had promised.

A body kin do what a body wants to—if a body wants to hard enough. She knew how to swim. She had to try. She kicked. She pulled with her arms, even as her lungs begged for air. She couldn't make the surface. Water saturated her wool uniform and its weight dragged her down. *I don't know if I can do it, Pap.*

She peeled off her blouse and jacket and struggled with her trousers, but couldn't get them off over her boots. She tugged at the boots until they came off and sank.

Her chest felt ready to explode with the need for air, and she pulled harder. Just when she thought there was no end to the water above her, she broke through the surface. She gasped. She breathed. And Given's piece of pine, Pap's knife, and Leander's pebble were gone. Forever.

Panting in the cold air, she saw the *Sultana's* lights in the distance. When she caught her breath, she swam toward the boat. It was downriver, so the current would help. She could reach it. She tried to ignore the frigid water that sucked what little warmth her body held.

The whoosh of the Mississippi's strong current filled her ears, but other sounds broke through.

Voices shouted, swore, hollered for help, screamed in pain. She looked toward the *Sultana*, where the lights were brighter now. Not just lights—fire! Steam hissed and the blaze sent burning debris into the night sky. And the water around the boat was alive! Men thrashed alongside the hull, hundreds of them. Still others jumped from the boat on top of those in the water, jumped from the decks, where flames lapped at their heels.

Polly swam toward them, but as she drew closer, a

man clutched at her arm, and they descended into the river's depths. She tried to pull him to the surface, but his panicked arms groped and clawed and threatened to drown them both.

Freeing herself from his grasp, Polly kicked and swam upward to breathe once more. The man was gone.

By the light of the *Sultana* and her flames, Polly saw more men who flailed in the water and grabbed hold of other men to stay afloat, only to have the Mississippi claim them all. Swimming into that mass of desperate men meant certain death. And Polly knew now that she wanted to live. She *had* to live.

Something brushed against her arm. She nearly pushed it away before she realized it was a piece of the very rail she had leaned against on the boat. Grabbing hold, she thrust her chest on top of it and let it keep her afloat as her arms weakened.

While she caught her breath, she looked for lights from the riverbank. The Arkansas side was closer, so she steered her piece of rail in that direction. She kicked and swam, just as she had often done back in the Coosa during her hospital days.

Debris floated close to her and she veered around smaller pieces. Might be she'd find something bigger than her rail, a piece she could climb onto to get out of the freezing water.

There! There was something big. It looked like a bag of clothing. Or a cushion.

But when Polly drew closer, she realized it was a man. Or what was left of him.

74

TREED

THE ARKANSAS BANK WAS FARTHER AWAY THAN IT looked. Polly kept swimming as the current pulled her closer and closer to the *Sultana* and her passengers, struggling in the water.

She floundered among dead bodies on the outer edge of the mass around the boat, and ducked away from living hands that clutched at her. Exertion overcame her. She needed to rest.

A few more kicks. She was away from men churning up the water. The current pulled her and her piece of rail farther downriver, until she could no longer hear the cries.

The lights of Memphis seemed to drift past her as if the city were floating, too. She'd have screamed for help if she'd had the strength. But it was too far away. And soon she had drifted past it.

Her mind drifted as well, in and out of darkness. She had to fight to keep the river from pulling her down into its depths. She had to swim. Again she pulled toward the Arkansas shore.

A shape loomed before her in the dark. It grabbed her by her drawers and wouldn't let go. She struggled to get away, lest she be pulled under.

"Let me go!" she cried, swinging her fists at the dark form. When her fist connected, she realized it wasn't a *someone*. She had been snagged on the branch of a cottonwood tree partially submerged in flood water.

She scrambled up into its branches. Bark scratched her feet, but she was finally out of the water. The night air chilled her through her wet drawers, and she shivered. Curling up in a notch of the tree, she tried to get her teeth to stop chattering.

Would the ordeal of the last ten months never end? All those men in the water around the *Sultana* had already been through more hell than the devil himself. They had thought their misery was over at last—and now, for most of them, it likely was.

It had almost been over for Polly, but she hadn't let the river take her. Now she wasn't ready to give up. She had fought her way out of the water once, and was determined to stay out.

But she was so very cold, and her eyes wanted to close. She fought them open, fearful they would close forever. Waves lapped against the tree trunk, and their sound tried to pull her in.

75

NIGHTMARES

S HE WAS DROWNING IN THE MISSISSIPPI'S BLACK WATER, water swirling with debris. The debris turned into men who clutched at her, trying to save themselves. She kicked them away as they screamed and begged her to save them.

Flames leaped high in the air and consumed the Sultana. The smokestacks fell onto what was left of the hurricane deck. And the river pulled her closer to the tumult, so close she heard the voices of the dying.

She swam away, swam and swam, but got nowhere.

Ducking beneath the surface, she let the freezing current pull her. She struggled to emerge, gasped for breath, and grabbed hold of a branch.

Lights floated by, blurring and disappearing. People stood on shore and watched her drown. No one came to rescue her. The cold seeped inside her and froze her blood. Her arms and legs turned to ice.

Someone touched her shoulder. She startled awake and stifled a scream.

"Miss, your stop is coming up directly." Not a panicked voice from her nightmare, this voice was friendly.

She looked up at the kind face beneath a uniform cap and reminded herself the nightmare was over. The prison was hundreds of miles away, the war had ended, and she had survived the horror of the *Sultana's* explosion.

She had been plucked from that cottonwood into a small boat by a boy who had taken her home to his folks. The Swains. They had warmed her and fed her hot soup. She had lain in a warm bed for weeks, while her strength returned. The first time she stood, her legs had forgotten how to carry her weight. She wasn't able to walk for several more days.

The Swains had told her about the steamboat disaster, how its boilers had exploded. She recalled how Bull had sought the warmth of the boiler deck, and she reckoned he had died. The Swains said the list of dead was more than a thousand names long. Surely Given's name was on that list. She needed to find his kin to let them know he hadn't been aboard.

★ ★ ★

The Swains had given Polly clothes to wear. Girl's clothes.

When she'd been rescued in drenched drawers, her true gender was no longer a secret. They had paid her fare to Ohio and now she was aboard a train for Ironton, a town near Hanging Rock, close to Given's home.

The prison, the explosion, and the icy river returned to her in nightmares most every night. But the nightmare she never woke up from was the one she'd have to live with. She was an orphan girl with no home.

After she delivered the message to Given's folks, she'd have to get hold of boy's clothes again. She'd have to find work, get a job to feed her and put a roof over her head. She didn't need much. After Andersonville, she could tolerate anything.

76

GETTING CLOSER

THE TRAIN STOPPED IN IRONTON, OHIO.

"This is your stop, Miss," the conductor said.

Polly was trying to get used to being called *Miss*, trying to get used to wearing a dress and bonnet.

She picked up her small satchel, but a man in a railroad uniform took it from her. "I'll get that, Miss."

Another uniformed man offered his hand to help her down the car's steps to the wooden platform. Being treated like a girl felt strange. And walking in women's shoes wasn't easy. She'd grown used to boots, familiar boots that were now on the bottom of the Mississippi River—along with Pap's knife, Leander's pebble, and that piece of pine, whose burns and scratches marked her days.

Inside the depot, she asked a man where to find the family of Given McGlade.

The man glanced at a clock on the wall. "If you hurry to Doc Marting's office, you might can catch a ride to the McGlade place. Doc heads out that way every Saturday." He pointed. "Down the end of the block, turn right, second door. That's where you'll find Doc. Hurry on now before you miss him."

She snatched up her satchel and hurried to the doctor's office. No one answered her knock on the door. Maybe she'd already missed a ride with the doctor. She knocked again.

"Come in," a voice hollered from the other side of the door. "Come in."

She opened the door to find a young man seated at a table.

"Sorry," the young man said. "I can't get to the door. Doc already loaded my chair on his buggy."

His *chair?* Polly didn't understand.

"I'm Polly Settles," she began, "from West Virginny. I'm lookin' fer the kin of Given McGlade."

"Given?" He squinted at Polly. "How do you know Given?"

Given had trusted her to take his message to his folks. She wasn't going to spill his secret to this stranger.

"I met him in Georgia," was all she said.

The door opened behind her and a tall man with spectacles filled the doorway.

"Your chair's in—sorry, I didn't know we had another patient. May I help you, Miss?"

"She's from West Virginia, Doc," the young man said. "Says she met Giv in Georgia, and she's trying to find his family."

"Feller at the train depot said might be ya'd take me to 'em," Polly said.

"I'm Doctor Marting. And I'm about to take Nate here to the McGlade house to see Given's sister."

"Lila," Polly said.

"How do you know her name?" the young man named Nate asked.

"Given told me."

"My buggy's out front." The doctor leaned down in front of Nate, and Nate latched onto his back the way Polly had with Pap when she was a young'un. "Follow us," the doctor said.

A number of patients at the hospital in Rome had lost the use of their legs. So had many prisoners at Andersonville. Had Nate been in the war, too?

A sleek black horse was hitched to the buggy, and Nate

climbed from the doctor's back to the footboard. Quick as a frog leaping into a pond, Nate's hands raised himself up and, in three precise movements, hoisted himself to the buggy seat.

That's when Polly noticed the contraption tied on the back of the buggy—a chair with wheels!

The doctor offered his hand to Polly to help her up to the footboard. She settled on the seat next to Nate, and the doctor climbed up beside her.

"I didn't catch your name, Miss," Doc said.

"Polly Settles."

"Given's letters didn't mention anyone named Polly," Nate said. "What did he tell you about Lila?"

"He said Lila's his sister. Told me his pap's a shoemaker. Said he's from Lawrence County, Ohio, not far from Hanging Rock. And he give me a message fer his kin."

"We got word the steamboat bringing Given home had an accident," Nate said. "I suppose you heard about that."

An accident? she thought. A whitewashed way to describe the horrid scene that dwelt in her nightmares. "I know about the *Sultana's* explosion," she said. *More than you'll ever know.*

Nate looked at her with suspicion. "And you saw Given's name on the list of *Sultana* dead?"

"No, but I reckoned it was there."

"You met him before he was captured and put in prison?"

Polly lied with a nod. Ever since that day Pap christened her Paul in the waters of the Kanawha, she had lived one lie after another. She wondered if life would ever let her stop. She would tell the truth to Given's folks. But they had to be the first to hear it.

"Given McGlade is . . . was my friend, and I'm a-needin' ta talk ta his kin."

Nate looked at Polly from the corner of his eye. "You claim to know so much about Given, but I suppose you ain't heard he wasn't on the *Sultana* after all."

Polly's mouth flew open. "What?"

They already knew he wasn't on board?

77
MEETING LILA

Y

"OU *KNOW* HE WASN'T ABOARD?" POLLY COULDN'T
believe it. She had come all this way to deliver a message,
but it had already been received.

"Must have been an army mistake," Nate said. "Their
roll showed him on board, but a letter came from him nigh
on ten days ago. He escaped from Rebel soldiers a few
months back."

Relief filled Polly. "So he did escape. I hoped he would."

With no message to deliver, what would she do now?
Where would she go? Given had said his mother would
take her in, but that had been months ago, back when
he reckoned she'd be mustered out of the army as Given
McGlade—if she even survived the prison.

Her inescapable daytime nightmare flooded over her. She
was an orphan girl with nowhere to go, no kin to live with.

She shook off that feeling and reminded herself that Given was alive. She had struggled for months to keep him that way. "Did he find Clara Grace?" she asked.

"How you know about her? Who *are* you?"

"Polly Settles," she said again. "Last I saw Given, he was on his way to find Clara Grace. He felt bad the Rebs burned her place down on account of him."

Nate looked at the doctor, and then at Polly. "We ain't heard none of that. Just that he escaped and does hired work for a girl named Clara Grace."

"It sounds like you have plenty to tell the McGlades," the doctor said, and clucked to his horse.

"It took quite some time for Giv's letter to get here," Nate said, "but I reckon he'll write again soon."

The buggy traveled out of town to a road that followed the river. Its water rushed past the buggy, and Polly looked away. She feared the memory of the *Sultana* explosion would be with her always. Right alongside those memories of the hell-place called Andersonville. How she wished she had stayed in Rome with Leander.

She hoped the McGlade house wasn't far. It was past noon, and she didn't know where she would spend the night. She had to get hold of boy's clothes and begin her search for a job.

★ ★ ★

At a house overlooking a pond, the doctor hopped down from the buggy and reached up his hand to Polly.

Before one of her feet touched the ground, a pretty blond girl appeared in the doorway. She smiled and hurried to the buggy.

"Did you have a good week, Nate? Your folks are coming to supper. Doc, can you get down his chair? Ma says you can stay, too, Doc, if you—"

She noticed Polly. "Oh, hello," she said. "I'm Lila."

"I'm Polly Settles."

"She met Given in Georgia," the doctor said.

"You know Giv?" the girl said. "How? When?"

"I met him afore he escaped from the Rebs," Polly said.

Lila's eyes opened wide. "Did you meet him before he was captured? Did you meet Leander, too?"

Polly found it hard to breathe. "Leander?"

78

LEANDER

*L*EANDER! In a moment like the first clear one after sun burns away a thick fog, images in Polly's mind made sense. At last, she remembered where she'd heard the name McGlade before she'd met Given. At the hospital, Leander had told her to let him know if a patient by that name came in. Leander knew Given! And Given's sister was named Lila, the same name as Leander's brother's girl! This Nate on the buggy seat must be Leander's brother!

She needed to hear him say it. "Are you Leander's brother?"

"I am. Are you saying you know Leander, too?"

She nodded. "Leander lost his arm in the war. Dang near died when they first brung him ta the hospital. But he pulled through. I writ a letter home fer him. Did he make it home?"

"He sure did," Doc said, "but he's not the same as the Leander who marched off. War changes folks."

"Like a river," Polly said. "My pap al'ys said folks is like rivers, ever a-changin' and ever a-changin' others." She pressed the dark side of rivers to the back of her mind.

"Leander doesn't talk about the war." Lila's mouth bunched into a pout. "He used to tell me everything, but he never mentioned *you*."

"He surely changed," Nate said. "A two-armed boy joined up, and a one-armed *man* came home. He works our farm harder than a mule. Ma tells him to slow down, but he says, 'A body can do what a body wants to, if—'"

"If a body wants to hard enough," Polly finished. Leander had remembered Pap's words!

Nate's face looked surprised. "You *do* know him."

She nodded. "And he's here? Now?" She could hardly breathe. Her heart seemed to thump right up in her throat. She'd been certain she'd never see him again. And now . . . Just the thought that he was close made his face clear to her. After all that time in Andersonville, trying to summon it to her mind. And there it was!

She looked up to see Nate's face scrunched with confusion. "I recollect the letter from Leander that was in

310

a different hand, the letter from the hospital in Georgia. *After* he left Given and the rest of their unit. How is it you met them both? Giv was never at that hospital."

"It's a long tale ta tell," she said. "And I scarce know where ta commence."

She tried to compose her muddled thoughts as the doctor untied the chair with wheels from the back of his buggy and lifted it down. By the time Nate was settled in the chair, a man and woman had joined the group gathered around her. The doctor introduced them as Given's folks. Polly's voice couldn't find the words she had prepared to tell them so long ago. They knew Given was alive, and the only words ringing through the confusion in her mind were *Leander's here.*

Everyone talked at once, and words pelted her ears like raindrops.

"Nice to meet you, Miss."

"Supper's on the stove."

"Nate's folks are comin' over."

Nate's folks are Leander's folks. Leander's here.

"Will you stay for supper, Doc?"

"How could I leave now and not hear the whole story?"

"I can take care of your horse."

"She's from West Virginia."

"She knows Given."

"*Says* she does."

"Plenty enough food for everyone."

"She brought word from Given."

"Word from Giv?"

"Giv was never at the hospital."

"You'll stay, won't you?"

"You have to stay."

"Lila, take her satchel upstairs."

"She knows Leander, too."

"Or so she says."

Leander's here.

"Put her in Given's room."

"She wrote a letter for Leander."

"And yonder he comes with Ma and Pa." Nate pointed.

Polly looked down a dusty path to see a man ambling beside a woman with a basket, her hand tucked tenderly into his arm. Just behind them walked a young man, whose empty right sleeve was tied in a knot near his shoulder.

"That's Leander," Lila said.

"I know," Polly said in a nervous breath. "I remember him." Even in the shadow of his hat's brim, Polly knew that face that had just now become clear again.

Leander looked up, and a faint trace of recognition flitted across his face. But nothing more.

He doesn't remember me, Polly thought. Tears pricked at the backs of her eyes. She'd been so sure their friendship had been as important to him as it had to her. But there was no sign of eagerness in his eyes at the sight of her. Had she meant nothing?

Of course he doesn't remember me, she realized. *He'd remember Paul.* She almost wished she were wearing her old army uniform. He had never seen her in a dress and bonnet. And her face was in the shade of that bonnet.

She untied the bow beneath her chin and let sunlight wash over her freckles and the red hair that had finally grown long enough to pull back in a ladylike bun.

Leander blinked rapidly as if his eyes were telling tall tales. He wiped his hand across them and blinked once more.

"Paul!" he cried, a grin spreading across his face, a grin wide enough to span the Coosa.

And Polly reckoned hers was even wider.

AUTHOR'S NOTE

AMERICAN HISTORY AND THE CIVIL WAR HAVE interested me since seventh grade. I read every book I could find on the subject. But several years ago, while visiting the Ohio River Museum in Marietta, Ohio, I learned about the *Sultana* disaster for the first time. It was hard to believe that a steamboat (built in my home city of Cincinnati) blew up and killed more people than died on the Titanic—and I had never heard of it! That was the first spark that led me to write this story.

While Leander Jordan, Given McGlade, and Polly Settles are fictional characters, their experiences were the kind lived by real people in the 1860s.

A young Union soldier stands with an American flag in front of a backdrop of a battle scene

315

Union soldiers pose by a supply tent. Officers' and surgeons' tents were this size, but enlisted men usually slept in small two-man tents.

Underage boys like Leander enlisted in the army. Records show that about 200,000 Union soldiers were sixteen or younger. The number who lied about their age and weren't caught will never be known. The Confederate Army had an even higher number of underage soldiers.

Like Polly, numerous women disguised themselves as men and fought side by side with their male counterparts. There are at least four hundred documented cases, but we can only guess at how many kept their secret forever.

The role of women in the 1860s was very different from women's lives today, and Polly had good reason to be concerned about her future after the war. An orphan girl would likely have been put in a home for girls or ended up on the street.

The mansion-turned-hospital in Rome, Georgia, where Polly worked and Leander was treated, was inspired by a real hospital. Civil War hospitals were often tent cities constructed wherever needed, but the army also took over homes and other buildings convenient to a battle site. Confederate Colonel Alfred Shorter's home in Rome was used as a hospital for Confederate wounded until 1863. The Union Army invaded Rome in the spring of 1864, and the Shorter home became a hospital for Union sick and wounded.

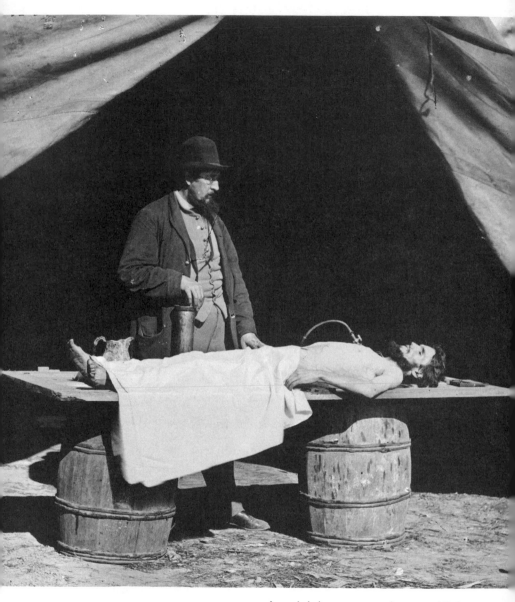

An embalming surgeon works on a soldier's body in a Civil War field hospital

Polly's unit came into the hospital sick from drinking contaminated water. This happened often. Disease caused twice as many Civil War deaths as battles did. Like Pap, men who lay in hospital beds for long periods often succumbed to pneumonia.

Leander's arm was amputated after his injury. In 1864, amputation was the only known way to deal with severe wounds. Fifty thousand Civil War survivors returned home as amputees.

When supplies failed to come through, soldiers were often permitted to *forage*, as Polly, Fox, Crawford, and Morgan did. Troops went to nearby farms and bought or stole food.

Sutlers were civilian peddlers who sold groceries and dry goods to the troops. They usually followed the army and set up a tent to display their wares when the army stopped to camp. Canned foods were still a recent innovation. Because spoilage was common with fresh food, canned items were big sellers for the sutlers. However, prices were severely inflated, and many soldiers couldn't afford to buy.

James Selman was a real sutler who had a lean-to inside the north gate at Andersonville's prison, like the one where Polly traded. Also like Polly's sutler, Selman closed up shop just before October 1, 1864, due to lack of business. He did return at a later date.

Camp Sumter, the real name of Andersonville's prison, is often referred to as "the infamous Andersonville Prison" because it became well-known for the atrocities suffered by its prisoners.

Accounts prove the shortage of rations. As Union troops moved into the South during the last year of the war, food became scarce. The Confederacy had trouble obtaining enough food to feed its own soldiers, much less thousands of prisoners. Union troops often stole food to feed their own army or burned warehouses to try to starve the South into surrendering. This added to the lack of sufficient food for prisoners.

The prison's unsanitary, crowded conditions and lack of adequate shelter and clean drinking water are also thoroughly documented. Photos exist of the open *sinks* over the stockade creek. The waste that dropped into the creek polluted its water, stank, and drew flies. There is little wonder that disease claimed thousands of lives at Andersonville.

The discovery of Providence Spring after a flood in August 1864 gave the prisoners access to clean water for the first time since the prison's earliest days. The spring is still there, but its water is no longer safe to drink.

The first prisoners were moved into the stockade in February 1864, before it was fully completed. Designed to hold 10,000 prisoners, the stockade's population reached its peak in August 1864, at around 33,000. About 45,000 prisoners altogether spent time in Camp Sumter.

Given told Polly his *shebang* had been used by prisoners with smallpox. The prison had a smallpox outbreak in early March 1864, and a pest house was built outside the stockade for its victims. Thousands of prisoners were vaccinated, but non-sterile practices of the time caused even more deaths. The last smallpox patient succumbed to the disease on July 4, 1864.

The dead-line was real, and men who crossed it were shot, but most who died in Andersonville were killed by disease, infected wounds, and malnutrition.

The hanging I described in Chapter 41 took place on July 11, 1864. As the fictional Given explained, the six "raiders" were tried, convicted, and executed at the will of their fellow prisoners. One of the condemned brandished a dagger in an attempt to escape before he was returned to the gallows.

& CO., LITHOGRAPHERS AND PRINTERS, BALTIMORE.

1. Head Quarters,
2. Rebel Camp.
3. Hospital,
4. Cook House,
5. Death House,
6. Death Line,
7. The Island,
8. Sutler's Camp,
9. Police Quarters.

ANDERSONV

AS

JOHN L

AUTHOR AND PUBLISHER OF "ANDERSONVI

WASHI

A print of Camp Sumter, also known as Andersonville's prison

COPYRIGHT SECURED BY J. L.

LLE PRISON

N BY

ANSOM,

IARY, ESCAPE AND LIST OF THE DEAD,"

ION. D. C.

10. Hospitals along the Death Lin
11. Market Street,
12. Broad Street,
13. Inside Stockade,
14. Second Line Stockade,
15. Third Line Stockade,
16. Lieut. Head Quarters,
17. Washing Place,
18. Rifle Pits,
19. Astor House Mess.

SEP 20 1862
No. 75013

Rumors of prisoner exchanges that never took place were common. Petitions to send to President Lincoln gathered many signatures, but no exchanges ever took place.

The new earthworks fort was real. When Union forces grew close, this fort was built as extra protection. It was called the Star Fort because its shape resembled a star.

Accounts tell of prisoners being moved to the south

The "sinks" (foreground) and shelters of
Camp Sumter as seen on August 17, 1864

side of the creek, like Given and Polly, where the sandy
ground made digging a tunnel unlikely. Accounts also
mention the practice of digging furrows in the sand for
sleeping in, and curling up together to share body warmth.

Like Bull, a large number of prisoners were taken to
other prisons in an attempt to ease the conditions at Camp
Sumter. Many thought they were being exchanged and

The execution of Henry Wirz, Confederate commandant of Camp Sumter, in Washington, DC, on November 10, 1865

were discouraged to find themselves in other prisons. Many were eventually returned to Andersonville, one group in a pouring rain a few days before Christmas.

Confederate Colonel J. G. O'Neil was a real person who inducted Union prisoners, like Given, into the Confederate Army when Southern troops were in short supply in the war's final year. His first attempt in November yielded only eight volunteers. After the harsh winter, nearly two hundred signed on.

When prisoners were marched out for release at Camp Fisk a mere thirteen months after the prison opened, burial trenches held about 13,000 bodies. The actual death toll is believed to be higher.

After the war, Captain Henry Wirz, the commandant of the prison, was tried for many of the deaths there. Convicted by a military tribunal, he was hanged in November 1865.

The Daughters of the Confederacy believed Wirz was a scapegoat. Records prove he was sick in bed when some of the deaths he was charged with occurred. In 1909, these women erected and dedicated a monument to Wirz, which still stands in the town of Andersonville.

Many of the emaciated prisoners from Andersonville, who were repatriated at Camp Fisk, were sent to Vicksburg and loaded aboard the steamboat *Sultana* to be sent home. There were also released prisoners from Cahaba Prison in Alabama and civilian passengers, including women and children.

The *Sultana* was built to hold 376 passengers and a crew of 85, but it was overloaded to carry around 2,500. The U.S. government paid the steamboat lines to carry their men home, and the *Sultana*'s owners' greed led to the vessel being overloaded. There was also a misunderstanding about how many men were actually being loaded. A photograph taken of the *Sultana* at Helena, Arkansas, shows these men

The *Sultana* in Helena, Arkansas, the day before she exploded and burned, April 27, 1865 who believed they were on their way home.

One of the *Sultana's* boilers had been patched when she was docked in Vicksburg, even though the steamer's chief engineer had recommended to replace it. Replacing it would have meant a delay, and the released prisoners would have been loaded on other steamboats. So the ill-fated journey began.

Around 2:00 a.m. on April 27, 1865, three of the boat's four boilers exploded, and she burned. Most of her passengers were lost, many burned or scalded from the boilers' water. Others were crushed in the decks' collapse or drowned in the Mississippi. Bodies were found in the water and along the banks for days. The number of dead from the *Sultana* explosion was nearly 1,800—almost 300 more than died on the Titanic nearly fifty years later. It remains America's worst maritime disaster.

But there were survivors, many of whom grabbed hold of debris from the explosion to stay afloat in the cold water until they were rescued. Several survivors made it to the branches of submerged trees until rescue boats came.

Some of the officials who had allowed the boat to be overloaded were arraigned in court, and one officer was court-martialed. A commission was assigned to investigate the incident and they heard testimony, but no one was ever punished.

If you haven't heard about the *Sultana* before, you might wonder why. News of the day included the end of the nation's bloodiest war, the assassination of President Lincoln, and the search for his assassins. The front page of the *Cincinnati Daily Times* on April 29, 1865, first reported the explosion with a small article. The same page also held reports of assassin John Wilkes Booth's death three days before and the arrival of Lincoln's funeral train in Cleveland.

After a war that killed more than 600,000, death had become commonplace, and few families were untouched by grief. Most large-city newspapers in the East gave little mention to the *Sultana* disaster once they learned the dead were almost entirely enlisted men from the Midwest.

Nearly 800 men aboard the *Sultana* were from Ohio, more than from any other state. There were also many victims from Tennessee, Indiana, Michigan, and Kentucky.

The country mourned collectively for Lincoln, but during the war and after the *Sultana* disaster, families in every state mourned individually for loved ones who never came home.

ACKNOWLEDGMENTS

A novel is not just written. It begins as a spark of an idea, which is fanned into a story plan. That plan is researched and mapped out. Characters are created, molded, fully developed, and given voices. Scenes are drafted and built into chapters. A narrative is constructed, composed, goaded, guided, strengthened, tightened, deepened, rewritten, revised, and tweaked. It took an army to help me accomplish this.

My army included Kent Brown and the Highlights Foundation's writers' workshops, which helped me to stretch my writing muscles and grow as a writer. I owe a debt of gratitude to many of their faculty members, including:

Rich Wallace, whose advice led me to rethink my characters and enabled me to shape the beginnings of this novel into the story it became.

Julie Ham, whose suggestions helped me to re-envision the story and work through the transition from Part One to Part Two.

Tami Lewis Brown, who convinced me that my words were worth reading.

Editor Carolyn Yoder, who took an interest in my story

and knew which questions to ask, making me rethink, flesh out my characters, and strengthen my words.

My fellow writers at the workshops, who added encouragement, which helped push me forward.

★ ★ ★

Accuracy in historical fiction requires being able to insert myself into minds from a time long past. That takes guidance from experts in many fields. I owe great thanks to:

Captain Tom Dietz, District Chief of EMS, Fire and EMS, Green Twp., Ohio, who helped to get my nearly drowned character Nate breathing again, using only methods employed in 1863.

Jim DeReamer, who taught me to load and fire a muzzle-loader like the one Leander would have used.

Toby and Ben Wiechman, whose knowledge of military practices and weapons was invaluable.

Rudy Clark, who introduced me to the Shorter mansion in Rome, Georgia, and gave me a tour of the antebellum home once used as a Civil War hospital.

The staff at the POW Museum at the site of Andersonville's prison, who answered my questions and directed me to the best research material on the subject.

Folks at the Steamboat Museum in Memphis, Tennessee, and the Ohio River Museum in Marietta, Ohio, for sharing their knowledge of steamboats and rivers.

Howard Wells, who shared his family's information on his great-great-grandfather, Jacob Zimmerman, who survived Andersonville's Prison and the *Sultana* disaster.

★ ★ ★

I also must thank:

The late Linda Sanders-Wells, who reminded me of the importance of telling this story.

My sister Reene, who is often my first reader and always my number-one fan.

My critique partners, Sandra Neil Wallace and Nora MacFarlane, whose feedback on Part One helped me to strengthen it and move on to Part Two.

The numerous members of my two critique groups. I wish I could list all their names, their helpful comments, and the ways they kept me on track throughout the process.

Swagger members Kim Van Sickler and Melissa Kline, who helped me work through the ending of this story.

Three women who inspire me daily: Kelly Broxterman, Wendy Rollinger, and Gina Gort. Like Polly, they survive life's trials with brave faces and find reasons to smile.

My personal cheerleader, Juliet Bond, who made me believe in myself and never let me give up.

And especially, dear friends Jon and Patty Egan, who sat for hours, listening to me read rough chapter after rough chapter. Their encouragement made it easy to keep going.

Most of all, I thank my husband, Jim, who accompanied me on research trips and who volunteered to shoulder the full financial burden of our family, so I could follow my dream to write novels.

SELECTED BIBLIOGRAPHY

Bull, Rice C. *Soldiering: The Civil War Diary of Rice C. Bull.* Edited by Jack K. Bauer. New York: Berkley Books, 1988.

Catton, Bruce. *The American Heritage Picture History of the Civil War.* New York: Random House, 1960.

Davis, Kenneth C. *Don't Know Much About the Civil War: Everything You Need to Know about America's Greatest Conflict but Never Learned.* New York: Avon Books, 1997.

Denney, Robert E. *Civil War Prisons and Escapes: A Day-by-Day Chronicle.* New York: Sterling Publishing, 1993.

Drew, Ken. *Camp Sumter: The Pictorial History of Andersonville Prison.* Americus, GA: Good Image Printers, 1989.

Hall, Richard. *Patriots in Disguise: Women Warriors of the Civil War.* New York: Marlowe and Company, 1993.

Havighurst, Walter. *Voices on the River: The Story of the Mississippi Waterways.* New York: Simon & Schuster, 1964.

Hesseltine, William B. *Civil War Prisons*. Kent, OH: Kent State University Press, 1972.

Huffman, Alan. *Sultana*. New York: Harper, 2009.

Long, E. B., with Barbara Long. *The Civil War: Day by Day: An Almanac, 1861–1865*. Garden City, New York: Doubleday, 1971.

Marvel, William. *Andersonville: The Last Depot*. Chapel Hill: University of North Carolina Press, 1994.

Potter, Jerry O. *The Sultana Tragedy*. Gretna, LA: Pelican Publishing Company, 1992.

Rhodes, Robert Hunt (Editor). *All for the Union: The Civil War Diary and Letters of Elisha Hunt Rhodes*. New York: Orion Books, 1991.

Silvey, Anita. *I'll Pass for Your Comrade: Women Soldiers in the Civil War*. New York: Clarion Books, 2008.

Trudeau, Noah Andre. *Out of the Storm: The End of the Civil War, April–June, 1865*. Baton Rouge: Louisiana State University Press, 1995.

Vandiver, Frank E. *1001 Things Everyone Should Know About the Civil War*. Old Saybrook, CT: Konecky & Konecky, 1999.

PICTURE CREDITS

The Granger Collection, New York: 316, 318, 326.

Library of Congress, Prints and Photographs Division: LC-DIG-ppmsca-37389: 314; LC-DIG-pga-02585: 322–323; LC-DIG-ppmsca-33768: 324–325; LC-DIG-ppmsca-34001: 328–329.